Highlander's Portrait

A Highland Secrets Story

enchanted keepsakes:

highlander's portrait

a highland secrets story

a sexy scribblers novel

by

c.a. szarek

Enchanted Keepsakes:

Highlander's Portrait
C.A. Szarek

A Highland Secrets Story
A Sexy Scribbler's Novel

Edited by Fiona Campbell

Paper Dragon Publishing
North Richland Hills, TX

eBook ISBN: 978-1-941151-16-7
Print book ISBN: 978-1-941151-17-4

Published in the United States of America

First eBook Edition: October, 2016
First Print Edition: October, 2016

Second eBook Edition: September, 2023
Second Print Edition: September, 2023

Other Books by C.A. Szarek

<u>Highland Secrets Trilogy & Companions</u>—Historical Fantasy Romance

The Princess and The Laird (Highland Secrets Prequel)

The Tartan MP3 Player (Book One)

The Fae Ring (Book Two)

The Parchment Scroll (Book Three)

Highland Valentine (A Highland Secrets HEA Story)

Highlander's Portrait (A Highland Secrets Story)

<u>Highland Treasures</u>—Historical Fantasy Romance

Highland Oath (Book One)

Highland Essence (Book Two)

Highland Skies (Book Three)

<u>The King's Riders</u>—Fantasy Romance

Sword's Call (Book One)—*Also in Audio*

Love's Call (Book Two)—*Also in Audio*

Rogue's Call (Book Three)—*Also in Audio*

Fate's Call (A Novella from the World of the King's Riders)—*Also in Audio*

<u>Crossing Forces—Romantic Suspense</u>
Collision Force (Book One)—*Also in Audio*
Cole in Her Stocking (A Crossing Forces Christmas)—*FREE read!*
Chance Collision (Book Two)—*Also in Audio*
Calculated Collision (Book Three)—*Also in Audio*
Collision Control (Book Four)—*Also in Audio*
Weekend Collision (A Crossing Forces HEA Story)—*FREE read!*
Superior Collision (Book Five)—*Also in Audio*
Incendiary Collision (Book Six)—*Coming Soon!*

<u>The Giovanni</u>
King of Hearts (Book One)—*Also in Audio*
Queen of Diamonds (Book Two)—*Coming Soon!*

enchanted keepsakes

Brought to you by the Sexy Scribblers!

Make sure you don't miss any of the stories of lovers Korinna helps discover each other!

Legacy by Chanta Rand
Highlander's Portrait by C.A. Szarek
Maybe Tomorrow by Lynne Connelly
To Love's End by Kris Calvert
Timeless by Angie Daniels
If Wishes Were Earls by Luanna Stewart
Fortune's Fool by J.A. Coffey
Passion Awakened by Valerie Twombly
Stolen Hearts by Kishan Paul
Forever Starts Today by Anne Lange
Saving Grace by Aubrey Wynne
A Sixpence in Her Shoe by Lena Hart
Breathe for Me by Anna Albergucci

Dedication

This one's for my friend, Kira, who never fails to have an encouraging word or genuine excitement for my stories. Makes a girl feel like she can do this writing thing.

Foreword

the legend of enchanted keepsakes

"True love has no boundaries. It knows no space or time. Human or immortal, true love will always find you."

Legend spins a tale of Korinna, a beautiful witch. With loving parents who doted on her, she wanted for nothing. On her fifth birthday, tragedy struck when her mother became ill and was suddenly taken from her.

For two years, it was only Korinna and her father, until one day he fell in love. Her father married, and their family grew.

Korinna's copper curls and wide violet eyes were a contrast to her four siblings' raven locks and emerald gazes. The men showered her with attention while ignoring her sisters, stealing their chances for love and marriage. On her eighteenth birthday, her resentful stepmother placed a curse upon her.

Korinna would forever walk the earth, never finding her own true love.

Her desire to help others sent her time traveling through exotic lands, collecting keepsakes along the way. With her treasures in hand, she placed an enchantment upon each of them. It is said whoever possesses one of these trinkets will be blessed with true love.

So, remember, the next time you step into a small shop, take a close look around. Do you sense the magic?

If you happen to spot a beautiful redhead with sparkling violet eyes, it just might be Korinna, setting up shop in your town.

Take care, for the treasure that whispers to you — to lift it from its resting place and take it home — could lead you straight to your one true love.

chapter one

ashlyn sighed and glared at the laptop. She gritted her teeth at the stupid — *really flippin' stupid* — blinking cursor and resisted the urge to slam her computer shut. However, it wasn't the machine's fault the words wouldn't come. They just wouldn't.

Screaming didn't help. Neither did cursing. Or jumping on the bed.

Pulling her hair just gave her a headache.

Her agent was past being nice, and her publisher…well, to say they weren't *happy* was mild. Very *very* mild.

"*Fired* is more like it," she muttered.

"I thought you weren't supposed to work."

Kate's voice made her jump.

When Ashlyn looked up into the sea-green eyes of her best friend, she frowned. "Well, you see, books don't write themselves."

Her bestie rolled her eyes, and her head with it, making her auburn ponytail dance. She was dressed casually — for a poshy clothing designer — in jeans and a V-neck tee that had '*I make fashion trends*' spelled out in jewels and sequins.

Kate propped a shapely hip on the corner of the desk Ashlyn was sitting at. "Then why the hell are we here?" She gestured around the adorable cottage, with the antiques hanging on display and the handmade multicolored quilts on the neatly made side-by-side single beds.

Framed tartans were on display on the walls, clan names and mottos hanging from wooden plaques underneath each, strung together with tiny chains. Clans from their current geographical location, according to the owner of the place their tour group was staying.

"Inspiration," Ashlyn forced out.

"So, you dragged me to the Scottish Highlands for..."

She tried not to glare. Didn't need crap from Kate, too. "You know, you're a lot like the heroine in this stupid book, who is obviously allergic to *happily ever after*. A pain in the ass."

Her friend smirked. "Maybe she's irritated at you."

"Why? What did I do to her? I'm trying to give her an awesome life. A hot laird in her bed and a freaking castle."

Kate laughed. "I swear it doesn't matter how many times I hear you talk about your characters like real people, it still throws me off. They have meds for that. Voices in your head and such." She waggled her hand not far from Ashlyn's face.

Ashlyn narrowed her eyes. "The longer you stand there, the longer you risk one of two things." She shot two fingers high, but not in a peace sign. "I'm gonna hit you or…"

"Kill me off in one of your books." Her bestie laughed as she finished the familiar threat.

"Yeah, what kinda friend are you, anyway?" Ashlyn pouted.

Kate pulled the chair next to the desk and folded her curvy form into it gracefully. "The best. Of course. You know I love you, Ash. I let you drag me to Scotland when I have two runway shows next month, didn't I?" She cast her eyes upward, then met her gaze again. The playfulness in her expression was gone; her pretty seafoam eyes were serious. "I hate that you're struggling. But you can growl at your computer at home. Treat this trip like a vacation and it might actually, I dunno, help your writing."

"Or lack thereof."

"You know what I mean. Unblock the block, or whatever."

"Right. I've just about lost all hope."

Her friend shook her head and grabbed Ashlyn's hand. "The tour group might be full of writers, but you're the only famous one locked away. Everyone else is jotting notes, snapping pictures, taking in the sights, and plotting stories for later, not that I understand any of that shit."

"Semi-famous."

Kate grinned. "I said all that, and you only latched on to the part I give you shit about?"

Her best friend had been calling her 'semi-famous' since her eighth book had come out last fall, and Ashlyn had hit a few lists. Lists that let an author feel validated, but unfortunately, it didn't make writing the next book any easier.

It had excited her agent and publisher, of course. She'd hit a goal, and they saw dollar signs…more books, another series, but it just put her head in a vise. The pressure was stifling. Not to mention, affecting her writing.

"Remember, some of your colleagues were swooning over the fact you're here with them. Bank on that. Sign autographs or something. I know it's anti-author, but we came like a million miles. Socialize or something, for Godssakes."

Ashlyn rolled her eyes. "I socialize."

Kate gave her a long look that made her want to squirm.

She didn't bother contradicting her. Her bestie would jump on her in a second for BSing. Ashlyn wasn't introverted like a lot of authors, but she didn't get out much, even at home in Dallas.

Her best friend had moved to New York when her clothing line, *Kateour*, had taken off a few years before, and she didn't have other friends nearly as close as she was to Kate.

They talked all the time on the phone, and even

Zoom and FaceTime, but it wasn't the same as when they'd been roomies in their two-broke-girls Dallas loft.

Begging her to come on this trip was part *I-can't-do-this-alone* and part *I-miss-the-crap-out-of-you.*

Ashlyn sighed for the hundredth time that morning. A feat—since she'd only been up a few hours.

"The group is going on a shopping trip. Don't make me force you," Kate said.

"Shopping? Ugh." She wrinkled her nose.

Her friend shook her head. "You. Are. Going."

"But…*shopping.*"

"Dude, we're in Scotland."

Somewhere Ashlyn had always dreamed of going. *Right.* Kate didn't have to say it. Especially since she'd been locking herself away at every stop the tour had made so far.

They were only in this cottage overnight, then were heading north as a group. The trip was guided and planned extensively. They were hitting all the famous spots the country had to offer. They'd started in Edinburgh on day one and were now in Inverness until mid-afternoon the next day.

Ashlyn had been writing about historical Scotland and the clans for years and had hoped this trip would bring her books to life in a way research couldn't. She'd written a trilogy about Clan MacLeod of the Isle of Skye, and was most excited about seeing the clan's stronghold, Dunvegan, which would be the last stop on their trip. Not only was it still standing, but people lived in it. A real castle! The stuff of her dreams.

"You just want to play fashionista in another country."

Kate flashed a grin. "Maybe. The people of Scotland need my sense of style."

Ashlyn laughed.

Triumph crossed her bestie's expression. "C'mon, you know you have obligatory souvenirs to buy, anyway."

"You're right. I guess."

"Oh wow. Don't sound so happy about it."

She *hated* shopping. Bought most of her clothing online, even bras and panties. Kate had chastised her about that for years, too. Along with the fact she wore her clothes until they fell apart. Her closet was only about a third filled, which was an insult to all women, according to the couture fashion designer.

"We're only in Inverness tonight. When we go further into the Highlands, civilization will be few and far between, so let's go with the group and shop now. Please?"

"I think you're exaggerating about civilization, but fine. I'll go."

Kate's eyes lit up. She leaned over and kissed Ashlyn's cheek. "You won't regret it. I might even buy you something."

"Yeah, yeah."

Her friend jumped up, changed into really cute boots Ashlyn could never pull off, and ignored her lack of enthusiasm.

She frowned when Kate pulled her toward the little shop with, "Enchanted Keepsakes" painted on a large plaque in the window. It was written in big white calligraphy-style letters and didn't seem to have the ability to light up.

The items in the window display varied, shouting that the place would have mostly eclectic goods.

"Since when do you like antiques?" Ashlyn quipped.

"There're more than antiques in there. Let's go check it out!"

She studied the items in the window again. There was a large blue vase with a modern edge to it, and what looked to be an antique bicycle right beside it, but also a small display case with fancy jewelry on the other side of that. A black velvet or satin necklace and earring holder sat to the right of the small glass case, and it had a ruby and diamond set on it.

Things that didn't seem to fit together. Things that were un-Kate-like, to boot. Besides the jewels, anyway.

"Are you sure?" She hesitated, pulling against the grip on her wrist.

"Geeze, for a history buff, you're being weird. I thought you'd be all over something like this little store. It's like stepping into the past. You could put it in one of your books. Just look at it. It's quaint and adorable."

"That's what you said about the cottage," Ashlyn muttered. "Not very fashion designer of you."

Kate laughed. "I don't have to have *everything* couture. Let's go look around."

Even the bell that announced them opening the door was old school. The scent of ancient and new hit Ashlyn's senses and she inhaled. There were other fragrances too, like sandalwood and lavender, so maybe the shop sold incense as well.

The wood floors creaked as they moved forward, but that made her smile. It really *was* like going back in time in a way, and it was comforting. Enveloped her so she wanted to look at everything all at once—and there was a lot to take in.

It had a pleasant, homey feel that she'd been looking for since she'd come to Scotland. Funny how this little shop had given her what she'd been seeking all week. It drew her in, like a warm embrace.

Ashlyn let her eyes feast.

Tapestries that looked to be from all over the world, some canvas and some embroidered, were on display. There was a rack of rolled ones in front of that. A shelf of globes of all sizes grabbed her attention, from ones that appeared very old to a brand-new, bright blue one front and center.

In the corner, there were paintings. Some were

framed and leaning against the wall and each other, and prints were in a bin, each secured to cardboard backings. She spotted landscapes and portraits. Even a painting of a horse with a cat sitting on his wide back.

Kate left her side to go explore on her own.

Ashlyn heard her boots on the hardwood, sounding as if her friend had headed to the back of the store. She wandered to a glass case and scanned its contents. Like the front window, the shelves contained a plethora of items. More jewelry, from big, oversized rings that looked medieval, to a bank of single-stone diamond engagement rings, then lockets of various sizes laying in rows on shiny dark cloths.

Under those were some carved daggers and dirks, which also looked very old. Next was something Ashlyn loved — books. They were big and small, some lying open and some standing on end in a neat row, like they would on a bookshelf.

"Can I help you find something?"

A pleasant voice caught her attention.

It was odd, accent-less, as if the woman could be from anywhere, or everywhere. Definitely not the Scottish inflection she'd expected.

Ashlyn looked up to meet a pair of…violet eyes?

Yes, violet.

More purple than blue, and mesmerizing.

The woman's face was just as gorgeous as her eyes. Porcelain skin, flawless across her high cheekbones. Red lips that couldn't be a natural color, but she didn't spot any obvious makeup. She had long red hair, brighter in hue than Kate's. It was loose and cascaded to her waist in waves.

She wore a gown, and it shimmered in the light, making it seem neither blue, nor purple, but more like a mother-of-pearl finish that brought out those incredible eyes. It was timeless in style, and as ethereal as the woman herself.

Her beauty stunned Ashlyn speechless.

She smiled gently, as if the reaction happened all the time—and hell, it probably did.

"Did you spot anything you'd like to get a closer look at?" she asked.

The question was also gentle, and jarred Ashlyn from her frozen staring.

What a freaking idiot. She's gonna think you're a lesbian, and you're hitting on her!

Heat kissed her cheeks and scorched the back of her neck. Even her ears burned. "Ah, I'm just looking, but thank you."

"All right, please let me know if something catches your eye." The woman's face brightened, as if the prospect excited her.

Ashlyn forced a nod—like a dummy—and wanted to flee the counter. Or melt into it. Maybe she'd locked herself away so much trying to write, she'd lost skills to function in public. She was socially inept, after all.

Ashlyn turned on her heel and slipped away from

the woman.

The paintings beckoned, so she headed there, looking first at a landscape done in pastels that dominated the wall in front of her. It was Thomas Kincaid-esque, but the only building was far off, a castle on a hill overlooking a grassy field and a pond.

She thumbed through the prints in the wooden bin. There were dragons, unicorns, other animals, and more landscapes.

Ashlyn stopped at all the castles, studying them to determine if they were Scottish or English, or from other places in Europe. All seemed to be real places, and some of the prints looked old, but some modern; some were even photographs.

There was even a painting of a castle she recognized as Vlad the Impaler's home, in Romania. She shuddered and shook her head. Who would want *that*?

This place had something for everyone.

Next to the large bin and the stacked framed paintings, was a small metal circular rack. It had all sorts of things on it—greeting cards, postcards, as well as funny sayings on small plaques. It was the first thing she'd consider touristy in the shop.

Ashlyn turned the display and it squeaked. She almost jumped, then yelled at herself for being startled. Her shoe bumped the rack's base, and it shook, like the whole thing could tip over. She winced and stilled it with one hand, but she could feel the tremors beneath her fingertips, like it was fighting her.

Movement caught her eye when something floated to the planked floor.

She bent to retrieve it when it hit with a soft *thud*.

It was a small piece of canvas, no bigger than a postcard, and its fragility was immediately apparent. She turned it over in her hands, trying to be as careful as she could.

Bright blue eyes peered up at her, and Ashlyn's gaze darted over his face. A portrait. He was handsome, with long dark hair that graced his shoulders. He was clean-shaven, which drew her even more when she scanned his strong jaw and chiseled features.

The painting only consisted of his head and shoulders, like a bust, but the recognizable MacLeod tartan pattern was slung over one shoulder, held up with his clan brooch. It was too small to make out, but the clan's motto, "Hold Fast," would no doubt be etched on it.

The detail and clarity of the image belied the age of the piece, Ashlyn guessed. She couldn't look away from the painted blue eyes. The man was gorgeous, and the small canvas took her breath, which was so silly, but it captivated her. "Wow," she whispered.

"What do you have there?" The redheaded woman appeared by her side, that pleasant smile on her full mouth, those violet eyes twinkling.

"I-I-I...found this."

Stuttering? Really?

Ashlyn held the painting out to who she assumed was the shop's owner.

"Oh my! How did this get here?" Her red-orange brow knitted, and she took the canvas with a soft touch. "I'm glad it wasn't damaged. Let me frame this for you."

"Ah, wait, I—"

The woman whirled away, her gown twirling around her as she sauntered to the counter and ignored Ashlyn's protest.

I never said I wanted it.

She *did.*

Ashlyn wanted to stare at it again. Study the sapphire eyes and the handsome details of his face. Even look at the portion of his ivory shirt visible, as well as the MacLeod plaid.

He would've been wearing a kilt, her gut said, if that part of him had been painted, too.

She went back to the glass showcase, where the redhead was humming to herself as she looked through a basket of frames.

"Hmmm, shall we go with gilt for Eoin?"

"Eoin?" Ashlyn whispered.

The woman nodded and her smile widened. "This is a portrait of Eoin MacLeod. Laird MacLeod in the mid-1700s."

The historian in her perked awake. "Where can I find out more about him?"

The woman held up an engraved gold frame. It was gilt-style, as she'd mentioned. "This is perfect!" She flashed a grin that Ashlyn didn't doubt could bring any man to his knees. "This is the one." She didn't answer Ashlyn's query, just handled the small canvas like an expert. Still humming, too. "Try not to touch the painting, all right? It's old…" She laughed.

Kate made her jump when she came to the counter. "Did you find something?" her bestie asked.

Ashlyn peeled her eyes away from watching the shopkeeper work, but she didn't want to. She wanted to catalogue what the redhead was doing with Eoin MacLeod's painting. Then she wanted to look at it again.

Her friend smiled and held up a pair of red jeweled Renaissance ladies' slippers in her hands. "I did, see?"

"Wow."

"That doesn't sound like a good wow," she pouted. "I'm not gonna wear them. I'm gonna plan a design or two. Maybe make a gown to go with something like this. Or branch out into a line of shoes. Been wanting to do that forever. This trip is for inspy, right?" Kate waggled her eyebrows and hugged the shoes to her bosom.

Ashlyn laughed. "I guess so."

"So, what'd you find?" Her seafoam eyes lit up.

"Ah, a painting." For some reason, she didn't want to share her find, not even with Kate.

"A painting?"

She ignored her friend's frown and glued her gaze back to the redheaded beauty. Her long hair swayed with her movements, but it wasn't more than a second before she held the small painting up, snug in its new frame.

"Here you go! I trust you'll take care of him."

Kate said something, but Ashlyn tuned her out and retrieved the frame with both hands.

She needed to look at him again. His deep blue gaze compelled her to stare. She imagined his smile — since he wasn't in the painting.

It would be a great smile; one worth swooning over. He would sound yummy, too. A full brogue that'd make a girl's knees weak.

Like all her Scottish heroes, he'd call her *lass*.

"Well, he sure is hot." Kate peered down at the image, over her shoulder.

Ashlyn fought the urge to squeeze it against her, hide it from view.

"Geesh, doesn't someone have a new precious?" Her friend smirked.

"*You* wanted me to come in here." Ashlyn arched an eyebrow.

Kate flashed a grin, then looked at the owner of Enchanted Keepsakes. "What do we owe you?"

Enchanted Keepsakes, indeed.

Ashlyn was certainly enchanted with the painting of Eoin MacLeod. She grinned and hugged the small frame; didn't care if Kate teased her.

She felt a story coming on, finally! She'd write Eoin MacLeod's love story. She didn't need to know about his real life — although the research might be fun.

Ashlyn would give him a true love in her current stubborn heroine. The storyline was still unplanned enough to change things around without starting over. She hadn't gotten too much into the hero's head anyway. Maybe the chick would cooperate if Eoin was her hero. He was hot enough.

Excitement bubbled up from her tummy. "We have to go back to the cottage," she told Kate as they exited the small shop.

"Now? Why?"

"I can finally write!"

Her friend giggled. "See? All it took was a hottie. Toldja!" Kate winked. "Too bad he's not real."

"Sure, he's real, he was a laird. A real person."

The redhead arched a groomed auburn eyebrow. "Well, the problem with that sentence is, '*was.*' Maybe we should go to the pub, and you can get *inspiration* from a '*now*' instead of a '*was.*' Like a real Highlander, ya know? They're still tall and hot."

Ashlyn shook her head. "Let me start with the '*was*' guy for now. Get some words down. Then I'll go with you. Promise."

Her bestie snorted but didn't answer.

chapter two

Prickles shot down his spine, making him sit taller. He paused, the quill hovering over the parchment he'd been writing on. Eoin waited, trying to judge if magic had kissed him, or if it'd been his imagination.

The shiver started again, in waves, getting stronger as the call was repeated.

Nothing was normal about the sensation. It wasn't a chill from a fire going out or a too-breezy room from gales outside. It was what he called, *'Fae-feels.'*

It was the telltale sign that it'd changed hands.

Again.

Korinna had promised she'd keep it safe when Eoin had entrusted it to her three years ago. Well, at least, three of *his* years. She'd told him he wouldn't have to go traipsing through the centuries to protect it. He could stay home in 1752—1755 now—where he belonged.

She'd ensured that a convincing-looking fake was put in its place, and even his clan didn't know. He wouldn't have to worry about what he didn't have control over—where the Faery Flag was in the far future.

Well, then, why the Fae-feels?

Eoin growled and made a fist. "I'm goin' ta kill that witch." He slammed the quill down. The inkwell on his desk jumped and spewed black ichor, as if in protest. It dotted the corner of the missive he'd been drafting.

He wiped what wetness he could away, but the letters were smeared, and the date he'd noted on the top right corner was obscured. He frowned because his skin was stained now, too.

"Somethin' wrong, brother?" Fiona caressed the doorframe of his ledger room for a moment before sauntering inside, making her skirts dance. She was dressed in finery, complete with a MacLeod plaid around her waist and tacked over her shoulder with a brooch he'd given her — a more feminine version of his own. Her ebony hair was braided intricately and pinned up, the ends framing her pretty face in cascading curls.

He wracked his brain. Had he forgotten about a feast of some sort?

It wasn't the anniversary of her birth — or his, for that matter.

Never mind.

Eoin wouldn't ask. The lass often sought attention, so that must be what this was about. He didn't bother chiding his sister about entering his sanctuary uninvited; Fiona didn't often obey him, even with the threat of bodily harm. Not that he'd put his hands on her — of which she was well aware. To his detriment, and it only added to her boldness. If she were younger, he'd tan her hide, but she was no longer a bairn.

"Nay." It came out a near bark.

Fiona arched a dark eyebrow. "Nay? Yer countenance states otha'wise, my laird."

He focused on her face, narrowing his eyes. "What do ye wan'?" His sister never addressed him properly unless she was begging for something. Dealing with the little pest of seven and ten would distract Eoin from his impending departure, anyway.

She smiled her most persuasive grin. The one that always melted their grandfather into a pile of goo, baring her right dimple and all the teeth in her head. She'd mastered the art of making her eyes sparkle to go along with it by her second summer.

Eoin had always been immune to that smile, despite his younger sibling's beautiful visage. It'd always led to her pouting, but he didn't respond to that, either. Everyone else in their clan doted on her; he couldn't afford to.

"Why would ye think I wanted anathin', except ta pay my respects ta my favorite brother?"

He picked up his quill and resumed his letter. The Fae-feels plagued his spine, but he wouldn't shift in his chair in front of his beloved little bother. He'd not have her thinking him weak for something she didn't know about. "I'm yer *only* brother," he said, not hiding the dryness of his words.

"Dinnae mean I adore ye any less!"

When Eoin looked up, his sister had curtseyed with a flourish, and her sapphire eyes were fairly shining.

"What. Do. Ye. Want, Fiona MacLeod?"

"Och, verra well, if ye need ta be as such." She flopped down into the chair nearest his desk, slumping her shoulders. Her bottom lip shot out in its familiar form. Her posture belied her garments.

Eoin studied her.

Fiona straightened her shoulders when she noticed. She took a breath, making her breasts heave and it occurred to him the green gown, made of glimmering fabric, was too low cut, revealing too much of her body.

When had she grown up so much?

She'd always been a pretty little thing, flitting around Dunvegan. Causing trouble, no doubt, but making everyone adore her, as well.

"Cover yerself," he growled.

His sister frowned. "Why? 'Tis the style. Ye approved a' this gown when I had it made, dinnae?"

He hadn't actually paid attention when she'd sought coin for new clothing. Something Eoin wouldn't make the same mistake about again. "Why have ye come ta see me?"

"I wish ta be wed," she blurted.

Eoin blinked.

His sister's fair skin flushed pink from chin to ear. She fidgeted in the oversized carved chair and wrung her hands on her lap.

"Aye?"

Fiona nodded, making the curls dance around her cheeks.

He'd thought he'd have more time to find her a suitable husband. Their father had passed when he was a lad, right before her birth, so the duty fell to Eoin as laird, but he'd been waiting for her to grow up. Not in years, but in maturity. "Verra well, I'll start tha search—"

"I ken who I want ta marry." Another blurt, and now her face was crimson.

"Who has put his hands on ye?" he snarled. He stood to his full height and rounded his desk, towering over his sister.

Her blue eyes went wide, and she shook her head. "Nay. Dinnae be—." Fiona retreated, cowering like she hadn't—ever.

"Then, explain ta me, Fiona MacLeod, *what* 'tis it *like*?" Eoin sat on the edge of his desk, only a few feet from her.

"He loves me."

His instinct was to scoff, but a silly smile lit his sister's face, and her eyes went glassy, what the lasses would call, *dreamy*.

"I shall kill him," Eoin declared.

Fiona focused on his face and glared.

Ah, there's my sister.

"Nay. Ye shall no' harm him! I *will* marry Kenneth MacDonald."

He startled.

She couldn't have—

"What did ye say?" he barked. Crossed his arms over his chest.

Fiona straightened in the chair and squared her slim shoulders. "We love each other."

Eoin was torn between anger and laughter. "Ye are seven and ten. The lad dinnae be much older. What do *ye* ken a' love?"

His sister didn't pout, as expected. She sat taller, and her eyes flashed. "What do *ye*? Ye've never wed. How do ye ken more a' love than I?"

Love is for silly lasses.

It didn't matter what *he* thought about love.

Eoin wasn't going to say that aloud. He'd not want her to think he was more like a petulant child than she. "Ye dinnae be marryin' a MacDonald," he commanded, low and gruff.

His sister rolled her eyes and *tsked*. "Our clans dinnae be enemies ana longer."

It was true, a great aunt of theirs—by marriage— had wed the MacDonald laird, so they were technically kin, but Eoin wasn't going to admit that to the lass before him.

MacDonald and MacLeod avoided each other,

and he liked that just fine. As it'd always been.

Kenneth was the current laird's heir, so if she married Callum MacDonald's son, his sister would maintain her station, but Eoin wouldn't give her to a MacDonald. "'Tis no matter. Yer no' goin' ta marry a MacDonald."

"I am so."

He narrowed his eyes. "Ye would defy yer laird?" His voice rose with each word, until he was shouting.

Of course, she would. She did so weekly, if not daily.

Frustration swirled in his gut and rose to his throat. He needed his grandfather, but then again, the man would probably side with the lass.

Eoin tried to use his size to intimidate her, but Fiona was on her feet now, her fists pinned tight to her sides, and she leaned toward him, as if her petite form could compete with his. Like most men in his family, he was well over six feet tall, and just as broad.

The material of her gown rustled as she pitched forward. Her eyes flung daggers at him.

If rage didn't dominate his body, he might've laughed.

"I'll run away!" Fiona shrieked. "We'll run away tagether."

Not likely.

The lad was the heir. He wouldn't.

"Kenneth vowed —"

"Is all well?" Jamie, the head MacLeod steward,

and their cousin poked his red head into the room. His eyes shot from lass to laird, and he cleared his throat, then shuffled forward. He inclined his head to them both.

The Fae-feels demanded all of Eoin's attention, making his body shake. He needed to get to the Faery Stones. The longer he waited, the more the demand would make itself known. He'd become ill if he resisted, and unable to walk.

He'd learned his lesson when he was a lad. Couldn't ignore the call. It was his duty to protect Clan MacLeod's Faery Flag.

"I've ta go now." He looked at Jamie, who was one of the few who knew of his duty and its demands. "The Flag calls."

"Ah. Verra well, my laird." The man, who was only a few years his senior, bowed. "Ye dinnae have ta fash when yer gone. Yer grandfa an' I shall handle clan matters."

Eoin fought a full body shudder and forced a nod. The magic that ran through his veins was screaming now. His heart thundered and his temples throbbed.

"What do ye mean?" Fiona yelled, but neither man acknowledged her.

He should have Jamie send someone to ready his horse, but he couldn't. If he wasn't there to keep an eye on his little pest, his steward would have to, because their grandfather would let her run amok.

Eoin cleared his throat and locked his gaze with

his sister's. So, she would know he was serious. Then he looked at their cousin. "Lady Fiona is ta be confined ta her chambers."

Her outrage was instant. Instead of sobbing, like most lasses would, she glared and started to holler at him. Even rushed to him and pounded tiny fists to his chest before he caught her wrists in a hard grasp.

A glare stopped Fiona from further assault, but she didn't close her mouth, uttering unladylike curses even after he'd released his hold.

Their parents would roll over in their graves to hear her speak as such. Even their grandfather would take her to task, were he in the room.

"'Twill be done, my laird," Jamie said, as if Fiona wasn't still screaming. "Safe journey."

"Thank ye, Jamie." Eoin pointed to his sister. "Ye, I *shall* deal with when I return."

chapter three

She closed her laptop and pushed back from the desk. Satisfaction washed over her for the first time in longer than she could remember.

Ashlyn had *worked*.

Written a few thousand words in less than two hours—probably a record for her, too. She didn't hate what she'd added to the manuscript, either. Certainly, a plus, especially with how things had been lately, concerning her and her chosen profession.

She felt *good*. Better than she had in months. Almost wanted to email Jayne, her agent.

Her gaze darted to the small painting she'd propped against the lamp next to her. Ashlyn locked onto Eoin MacLeod's sapphire eyes. His gorgeous, but stoic expression made her want to know something about him for real.

She'd made things up about the character she'd just invented based on him, but…Ashlyn craved facts about the real laird. Maybe *he'd* been the reason the story had flowed so well.

Stop being ridiculous.

"Are you done? Damn, your fingers were flying." Kate whistled in appreciation, looking up from the magazine she was perusing while lounging, stretched out on her bed.

Ashlyn jumped, couldn't help it.

Then cursed the eyebrow her bestie arched.

If she teased her about the painting, Ashlyn would deck her.

Kate hadn't stopped her best impression of Gollum since she'd seen Ashlyn treating the laird's image with kid-gloves.

She forced a nod. "Yes, I got them through the first kiss."

"Good stuff?"

"Hope so. Let you read it later." Her eyes found the laird's again, half against her will since her friend was most likely still watching.

What would it be like to kiss a man that looked like him?

It'd been a while since she'd kissed *anyone* — let alone done more than that.

Oh, God, just stop. It's a freaking painting.

Did Kate have a point with the "my precious" stuff?

Ashlyn fought a wince.

"Awesome. I love your stories."

She scoffed.

"I do, Ash! I just don't get to read. I'm a busy girl. Runway shows and production take up so much of my time. My average work week is seventy hours!" Her friend sighed. "If I get into *Marie Claire*, I'll be even busier." Kate sounded wistful. She wanted a spot in the magazine more than anything else—lately anyway.

"I know. Sorry I gave you crap. I appreciate all your support; you've been with me from the start," Ashlyn said, genuinely remorseful.

"Always, babe. I can say the same for you. I was a nothing designer longer than you were a nothing writer." She popped up and closed the distance between them, sliding an arm around Ashlyn's shoulders for a quick squeeze.

Ashlyn smiled up at her friend. Her bestie might be a pain sometimes, but she couldn't imagine life without her. It really sucked that they lived so far apart now. "What's next on the agenda?"

Kate grabbed the guide the tour personnel had given them all on day one from next to Ashlyn's laptop. She ran her finger down the color-coded time and date listings' table. "Looks like free time until eight. Then we're supposed to gather up out front for a ghost walk."

Ashlyn rolled her eyes. "Do we have to?"

"Oh yeah, I totally wanna go to that. But right now, you have a promise to fulfill."

"I do?"

Her friend perched a hand on her hip. "The pub, babe. The pub."

Ashlyn groaned. "Really?"

"Are you trying to spoil my fun again?"

"No, no. I'll go."

"Again. Don't sound so happy about it. Maybe I'll be able to snag me a hottie-Scottie." She waggled her auburn eyebrows and Ashlyn couldn't help but laugh.

"Well, you're not gonna bring him back here, I won't have any of that sock-doorknob stuff."

Her friend threw her head back and laughed, making her groomed ponytail dance. "Okay, that was *one* time, and in college; give a girl a break."

She smirked. "No way. I'm never gonna let you live it down. I got a *B* on my English mid-term because of you. My books were in our room, and I needed to freakin' study, dammit."

Kate's mouth fell open. "Seriously, Ash? The horror, a B! That was *ten* years ago. I don't even remember the guy's name."

"I do."

"Yeah?" Her friend's mouth rippled, like she was trying not to smile. She cocked her head to the side, waiting.

"That B traumatized me for life."

"More than the sock?" Her best friend snorted.

"Yeah. It burned images in my head forever. Brad-the-douche."

Kate wrinkled her nose. "Ugh. Him! Don't remind me. He *was* the hugest douche ever."

Ashlyn giggled. "He was pretty bad."

"I don't know what I saw in him."

"Told you that!" she said in a singsong voice that

made Kate roll her eyes.

"That's why being single is better."

"Thought you were gonna snag a hottie-Scottie?" Ashlyn shot back.

"Sure, to shag, not marry."

She shook her head as Kate flipped her suitcase open and started rummaging through her clothing. "I don't know how we're friends," Ashlyn teased.

"Well, only one of us can be the hopeless romantic. I guess it makes sense it's you, who makes up happily-ever-afters for a living."

Ashlyn's eyes cut to the painting of Eoin MacLeod. "Too bad they're made up."

Jesus, stop being an idiot.

"You say something?" Kate asked.

She met her bestie's green-blue eyes and shook her head. No way she'd admit her head was in the clouds. It was only something another writer could understand. Maybe she was still too hooked into her manuscript and her new hero.

Kate didn't bat an eye, just twirled in the very low-cut fire-engine red top she'd put on. Her bust was generous anyway, but the shirt gave her cleavage with a capital C. It was shimmery fabric that caught the light and had long billowy sheer sleeves. She'd also put on some tight black pants and a pair of red heels that were probably Louboutins. "How do I look?"

"A tad too rich for a neighborhood pub in Inverness."

"One always needs to look one's best. Especially someone as sexy as this *one*." Kate gestured to herself and winked. "Are you going to change?" The signature arched eyebrow suggested the question was more of an order.

Ashlyn stood and looked down at her navy tee that read, *"Writers have text appeal."* It was one of many nerdy shirts she owned—and loved. Her jeans were dark denim, and her favorite pair for how they hugged her hips and made her ass look smaller. "What's wrong with what I have on?"

Kate cast her eyes to the ceiling as if she was seeking divine intervention. "What am I gonna do with you?"

"Hey, this is my *vacation*, remember? As you so aptly pointed out." She flashed a grin. "I'm not supposed to have to get dolled up. Didn't bring fancy clothes, anyway."

"Of course, you didn't. And you're awesome, tossing words back in my face." Her bestie mock-glared.

"You're welcome." Ashlyn giggled.

"Well, let's go." Kate gestured to the small desk and made a face. "It'll be good to get you away from your new man, and maybe, just *maybe*, you can meet a real one. You could benefit from the company of a male that's not in your head."

Ashlyn stole a look at the painting but chose not to comment. Resisted the urge to stick her tongue out at Kate, even if she was right. She grabbed her tote embroidered with her name and slung it over her shoulder. It felt empty without her laptop inside, but she was done working and could definitely use a drink. Not like she'd write in a noisy pub, anyway.

She took a step toward the door, where Kate already was, then looked at Eoin MacLeod again, as if compelled.

"Ash, are you coming?"

She murmured a response, but her feet didn't move.

Her friend exited their room ahead of her, and Ashlyn darted back to the desk. She stared at the painting for a split-second, then slid it into her bag.

Eoin pulled on the uncomfortable modern trews. They were called *jeans* and were made of a material he'd learned was referred to as denim. He had no love for them, but he'd come forward in time on more occasions than he wanted to contemplate, and the tight garment seemed to stay relevant, no matter the year. He could blend in, which was essential.

He preferred his plaid. It allowed movement and comfort, but it seemed the men of his country only wore them for show in the future. It was a shame. A loss of culture.

Eoin tried to limit what of the future he retained. Knowledge made going home harder, especially since he couldn't share what he'd witnessed with anyone, except his grandfather, who already knew of wondrous things from his grandmother.

He'd seen marvels he'd not understood the first time he'd come forward, but that'd only changed with time, putting him in even more awe. Eoin knew the names of things, like automobiles and televisions, even the telephone, but he'd learned of mobile phones when he'd given his Flag to Korinna.

Wonders he couldn't begin to understand, but he no longer feared. The witch had helped with that, actually. He hadn't taken her as a lover, but he would've if she'd wished for the same. Her ethereal beauty was as timeless as she.

He pulled the soft blue shirt over his head. It was tight to his body, nothing like tunics or leines he wore in his own time. It was called a T-shirt, and he had both long and short-sleeved versions. This one had a pocket over his heart.

Eoin kept a variety of clothing stowed in a modern satchel, buried in the corner of the cave the Faery Stones were in, under rocks and sand. He'd gathered the things and left them there; he always had to undress before time traveling. The Stones stripped a person of everything but what was held in one's hands, but only when traversing centuries.

He'd left his plaid in the cave of 1755. When he got home, he wouldn't have to head back to Dunvegan naked. However, he'd brought his claymore with him through time, holding it in his hands for that purpose. He'd have to leave it in the cave of the Faery Stones, for this was a time when people didn't carry weapons openly, but he always felt better knowing it was there, awaiting him.

If he went to the Fae Realm in his own time, he'd keep his clothes and weapons—and Eoin would need his claymore, if not more than one. Winged Fae Warriors killed humans on sight, no matter what amount of Fae blood ran through his veins. His great-grandmother, Alana, had been a full-blooded Fae Princess.

He'd gone into the Realm of the Fae a few times as a lad and had barely gotten back to his home on the Isle of Skye on each occasion. He stayed away, learning his lesson. Had no reason to go there.

Eoin had an innate ability to know *when* he was in time; if he happened to come to a year before his supplies were present in the cave, he could always open the Stones again and go to the place in time when what he needed was there. That hadn't happened to him in a while, at least not since his last trip.

Instinct told him he was no more than three of his years in the future since he'd given the Flag to Korinna; it was the twenty-first century, and the farthest in the future he'd ever had to travel.

The Flag had changed hands many times since he'd planted the fake in the treasures of his clan, but he'd always been able to save it from causing damage.

He'd taken the real Flag back with him, but somehow it never worked, and he was always sucked forward after it again.

He had no control over it, and no choice but to answer the call. He was linked magically to the damn thing, and even when the real Faery Flag had been in Dunvegan with his ancestor Rory MacLeod's horn, and the Dunvegan Cup, he'd had to come to the future when the Flag ended up with a new owner.

Eoin didn't understand why it wasn't safely in modern-day Dunvegan. He'd been proud to learn that not only was his clan's stronghold still standing—his descendants occupied it, at least some of the time.

When Korinna had convinced him to give the Flag to her for safekeeping, and suggested he install a fake, the change of hands in the future made more sense, but it hadn't stopped things from reoccurring when he'd brought the real thing back to the past.

Puzzling, but not even the witch could explain the circle of time.

Eoin stuffed his feet into black boots and buried a modern *sgian dubh* he'd purchased on one of his trips inside it, tucking the short hilt against his ankle. He refused to go weaponless entirely, so this was an alternative he could handle. The knife was black-bladed, made of a fine material much better than anything in his time, but he couldn't bring it home with him.

Very few could know of his duty—or how he

fulfilled it. It was a secret role handed down to one chosen male MacLeod to another—not necessarily the laird. His grandfather had trained him, but before Eoin's grandfather, it'd been a cousin. Both older men had mentored him in one way or another.

The Fae magic in their blood varied, and the role of Guardian fell to the male with the most magic. He had the ability to *blink*. He could picture himself in a location and appear there. It took concentration and could wipe him out physically if he did it too many times in one day, but it was something he'd been able to do even as a wee lad.

His cousin—the grandson of a Fae Warrior that'd married a great-aunt of his—could do the trick as well and had helped Eoin hone the skill. His grandfather could *blink*, too, but the man had struggled with it the older he got, so he'd taught Eoin other Fae magic instead.

Eoin hadn't had to do any of this in three years, so he was rusty, anyway. Was going to have to rely on the magical tie to the Flag more than he should. The good thing was, if he concentrated, the Flag's magic would pull him to it, no matter *where* in the world it was.

It wasn't necessarily in Scotland. That'd only happened once. He'd had a scary experience in America, but back in the early twentieth century. In a place called New York City—a place he hoped to never see again.

He growled. He was going to have words with

that witch — if Korinna was still in Scotland. She moved around in time *and* place. Eoin had thought he was done chasing the Faery Flag. Trusted her to care for it. He could stay home, stay with his clan and family. Live his life. She'd assured him of it.

What happened?

He'd have to find out.

Eoin had only entrusted the Flag to Korinna in the first place because the witch had greater magic than his own. The Fae blood in the MacLeod line was diminishing. He worried that there wouldn't be a MacLeod after him who could feel magic or be tied to the Flag, but he'd been telling himself for years he couldn't dwell on it.

It wasn't like there was a Fae Princess volunteering to marry him, like his great-grandfather, Alex. Eoin couldn't saunter into the Fae Realm to seduce a female — princess or not — either. Human blood in the Fae Realm was a death sentence.

His sister didn't have any magic, and that scared him, too. If the blood wouldn't help his clan protect what was theirs, what would?

Eoin didn't have time to focus on that; he needed to go to the Flag.

Giving it to the witch had been a mistake. He'd failed in his duty.

His great-grandparents would roll over in their graves.

He buried the paper money in his back pocket.

Korinna had been helpful in explaining what modern currency was the first time he'd met her, as well as assisted in gathering his cache. He didn't know if he'd need it, or how much, but it might take him more than one day to ensure the Flag was safe.

His gaze swept the cave as he hid his satchel and sword. The Faery Stones glinted, as if some light source was present to reflect off the crystals, but the radiance came from inside each one. They gave off enough light to illuminate the cave, but they were hidden well enough to prevent unexpected guests. No one would find this cave unless they knew where to look.

The Faery Stones were made up of five clustered natural formations, rising from the cavern's floor, perfectly spaced from each other, in a loose semi-circle. One was centered, and the other four surrounded it.

Eoin's grandfather had long ago explained that the crystals atop the five pillars were from the Realm of the Fae, and magic-born. The one in the center was larger than the rest. It was the key to making the others work. They had to be in tune as a whole to open the portal.

The formation they sat in was perfect, as if it had been placed there, not grown. That was probably the case; they'd been put in the Human Realm a millennia ago by the Fae who'd wanted to link their worlds.

As Eoin stared, the main Stone called to him, brightening, and humming as if in welcome, even though he hadn't touched it. He had a strong link to the Stones and had been able to open them from the first time he'd tried, amazing both his grandfather and cousin.

"I know 'tis been a while since we've seen each other," he murmured. He couldn't caress the Stone, or the others, because the pattern required to open them was instinct, and he wasn't ready to go home.

Eoin clutched the medallion that hung low on his chest on a leather strap. Korinna had given it to him and disguised the natural magic inside it with the MacLeod seal affixed on the outside. Its properties prevented the suffering effects of hundreds of years of time travel that hit a person without it.

Before owning it, he'd woken time and again, wandering naked on the beach, disoriented from navigating the rift in time, and even though the Flag's magic always reached out and righted him, time travel was much preferred with the medallion.

He closed his eyes and took a breath. Needed to concentrate on the Faery Flag. Eoin pictured himself holding it, caressing the silky fabric, and running it through his fingers. It was made of the softest material, Fae in origin, and older than even his Fae great-grandmother.

Legend was, it'd saved his clan from disaster two times, and it only had one more wish left in it. He didn't know what he believed about that, since the supposed saviors were Fae, and most of the race hated humans, but the Flag definitely had magical properties.

It was a MacLeod treasure and he'd willingly given it away.

Eoin winced. His ancestors would never forgive him. He had to get it back, and somehow, this time, keep it. Prevent himself from having to traipse through time after it and maybe prevent the need for a new Guardian in the future. That would solve the dissipating magic worry.

The Flag's magic called to him with only minimal concentration.

Forcing another breath, he locked onto it with his mind, allowing his link to center him and fill in the blanks his brain needed to get to it, sight unseen.

"I have ye," he whispered.

Eoin smiled and *blinked*.

chapter four

ashlyn winced at the din in the small, crowded pub. She wanted to go outside — or go back to their cottage. The air was stale, like old whiskey and the scent of beer swirled around as tangible particles. The building was old, and it was as if she could smell the wood supports and exposed ceiling beams, maybe even the stone walls, too.

Somehow that had appeal, as much as she didn't want to admit it. It helped but didn't overcome the odor of too many bodies in a confined space, or the smoke in the place. Sweat, and some mustiness clung to everything, also tainting the air.

There were more cigars than cigarettes, but the various clouds still made her hold her breath when they drifted her way.

There was a soccer game playing on the three flat screen TVs that hung on the walls, and from time-to-time shouts or cheers from the mostly male patrons. Curses too, when things didn't go the favored team's way.

Scots took their football seriously.

Kate was in her element, of course, flirting with the bartender. Ashlyn had to hand it to her; he *was* pretty hot, although he didn't have Eoin MacLeod's sapphire eyes.

Oh my God. Seriously?

She resisted looking down at her bag, or worse, feeling around inside to convince herself the painting of the laird was still present and accounted for. Undamaged and *with* her. Like she *needed* it. After chiding herself some more, she looked back at the bartender.

His hair was brown, and he was tall. His black tee, emblazoned with the pub's logo, clung to his pecs, and hinted at hidden abs, it was so tight. His biceps were nice, almost too much for that clinging shirt. He had dimples, to boot. The accent was a magnet, and her bestie was fairly hanging on everything the dude said as they laughed and talked.

He was definitely romance novel hero material.

She's still not kicking me out of our damn room.

Ashlyn wrinkled her nose when a puff of smoke floated into her face. Her eyes watered and she blinked, clutching her bag tighter on her lap.

The smoking man passed too close for comfort, hollering at the bartender for a beer. His words slurred; it obviously wasn't his first. He sounded German, so he was likely another tourist like her, but it didn't give him any manners. She leaned forward until the edge of the bar bit into her tummy.

Soon, Mr. Hot-Barkeep had done his bidding and he retreated. Then hottie-Scottie went back to her friend, dimples showing before she'd even spoken again.

Ugh.

Pretty soon, Kate was going to be in what-time-do-you-get-off territory.

Still not sock-on-the-dooring me.

Ashlyn really needed some air. Her bestie was so involved in getting her flirt on, she wouldn't notice if she slipped out, so she'd do just that.

She slid off the barstool and turned, running smack-dab into a body. Her cheek hit a chest and she winced, because it was hard enough to be a shoulder. Stinging shot up her jaw and she fought the urge to close her eyes or call out.

Damn, that hurt!

She wobbled, but she couldn't drop her bag to keep from falling on her ass. Wouldn't risk the fragile painting inside.

A large hand swallowed her upper arm, steadying her.

The apology died on her lips when she looked up. Her mouth hung open, but Ashlyn snapped it shut as soon as it occurred to her, she was staring, dumbfounded.

"I am sorry. Are ye well?" The deep voice rushed over her like a caress, and she shivered in his grip.

He looks just like…

She swallowed and blinked. Had to be in her head.

It wasn't real.

Can't be real.

Maybe she'd hit his chest hard enough to scramble her brains.

"Lass?"

There it was.

The word.

Sounded just like she'd known it would.

Ashlyn jumped, snapping back into her skin.

Get it together. Now.

"I-I-I'm fine. Thanks for catching me."

He nodded, but his gaze—one that matched the royal blue T-shirt he wore—studied her face. "Yer American?" He released his hold on her, and she was cold without his touch.

She concentrated on his accent. It was just as gorgeous as the bartender's but in a different way. Unrefined, a true brogue. It sounded old. Like it would've years ago. Like in one of her books.

Way more appealing than the hot barkeep's.

He was looking at her expectantly.

Duh, he asked you a question.

"Yes, I am," Ashlyn managed, but it was fragmented.

If she wasn't seeing things, how could the man before her look that much like her painting?

She had to be misremembering the face she'd spent the last few hours memorizing. The man she'd based her new hero on, who'd lived three hundred years ago. Her character was too fresh in her thoughts.

This guy…it just *couldn't* be real. Had to be a mind trick, but it wasn't like she could dig out the laird's image to compare right then and there.

He'd think she was crazy.

He was super tall—had to be six-five or six-six, and her cheek already knew the muscles of his clinging tee were real. He had a leather necklace on, but whatever hung from it was tucked into his shirt. It was round though; she could see the outline of it.

The laird-lookalike was wearing jeans, and even though Ashlyn couldn't see his ass, instinct told her he had no issue filling them out.

She wanted to see.

"You look like—" she blurted, then slapped her hand over her mouth, keeping, *'my painting,'* from popping out. She shot a glance over her shoulder at Kate, but her bestie was still deep in conversation with the bartender.

Ashlyn pulled her bag into her chest and wrapped her arms around it. As if the man would grab it and see the image of Eoin MacLeod.

"Aye?" he prompted.

She shook her head. However, she couldn't help but study the planes of his face. He was chiseled there, like the rest of him; high cheekbones, strong jawline that had a five o'clock shadow creeping over his clear skin. So handsome it took her breath. Her mouth went dry, her tongue plastered to the roof of her mouth.

He was hot.

Way hotter than Mr. Barkeep.

Ashlyn wanted to run her fingers over his cheeks. Trace his lines.

The resemblance to Eoin MacLeod was uncanny, except this man's dark hair looked a little shorter than the laird's in the painting. The dude before her had a shaggy look, his sable locks teasing above his shoulders. Messy, but appealing.

She didn't really like guys with long hair — outside her books, of course — but this one pulled it off. As if he'd look odd with it all cut off. Ashlyn wanted to bury her hands in it, see if it was as soft as it looked.

He was staring; but so was she.

Double embarrassment. Perfect.

Heat kissed her cheeks, spreading up to her ears and around the back of her neck. She swallowed and shifted her feet. The stuffiness in the pub kicked up a notch. She wanted to suck in air but wasn't a fan of breathing the staleness deep. It wouldn't help. "If you'll excuse me, I was trying to go get some air."

He cocked his head to one side and narrowed his eyes. "I'll go wit' ye."

"Why?" The word rushed out.

He isn't a creepy stalker, is he?

She wanted to push past him, but he was solid, built like a linebacker. It wasn't like she'd get far if he didn't want her to.

Ashlyn gave him another once-over and a tremor

slid down her spine. It wasn't fear; it was awareness. Anticipation, as if she was drawn to him.

This guy wouldn't hurt her; her gut shouted that much.

However, why on earth would he want to follow her outside?

This lass had the Faery Flag?

How?

Eoin stared into the wide brown eyes of the bonnie American. The magic tying him to the treasure had never been wrong before, and the tug was definitely present. Throbbing, actually, as if he was right on top of it.

The Flag was close.

"'Tis late," he murmured an answer to her demand, and received a honey-colored furrowed brow as her answer. He didn't want to let her by him, and the pub was crowded, so until he moved the lass was stuck with him.

That pleased him somehow.

Eoin had *blinked* to Inverness. He'd recognized the city immediately, even though it looked vastly different from the Inverness he was used to in 1755. His magic had honed in on the place as soon as his booted feet had hit the cobbled street outside of it.

He'd known the pub for what it was quickly. Had studied the sign before entering and spent a time watching people come and go. Eoin had even contemplated ordering some ale, but he hadn't taken two steps inside before he'd felt the pull of the Flag and had headed toward it. He'd seen the lass' back turn just seconds before she'd collided with him.

He hadn't known *she* was the source of the magic's draw until their eyes had met for the first time. The Flag was calling to him like a beacon, and it was close to *her*.

Eoin couldn't help but stare. She was stunning. A heart-shaped face was complete with a pert little nose and a wide, inviting mouth. Fair skin, and freckles strewn across the bridge of her nose, noticeable despite the dim tavern, only added to her appeal. She was blonde, but it was the same rich honey hue of her eyebrows and fell to her shoulders in waves beckoning him to touch it.

Her attire was similar to his, a dark blue T-shirt and jeans. She had a massive satchel with bright colored ink splotches on the fabric, and she clutched the thing as if she had to protect it.

He hadn't had a woman in a while, but the allure to this one was like a tug of magic; strong. Desire hit him in the gut, and he wanted to lean down and taste her mouth.

Nay. Doesn't make sense.

Eoin needed to get the Flag and get home, not be thinking with his cock. He'd never taken a lover from the future, although he'd realized early on during his travels that lasses of what Korinna called, "modern days" were different than females of his time. More open to the casual intimate company of a man, but they weren't whores at a brothel.

"Can you move?" she asked. Her brow was still knitted, despite staring at him. She was irritated, but her cheeks were crimson, and that enticed him, too.

Eoin shook his head. "I'll accompany ye, as I'd said."

"Why?" the lass repeated. She held the satchel higher; tighter.

His eyes brushed it, and magic screamed in his head.

The Flag was inside the thing.

She couldn't know what he sought, could she?

Why was she so defensive of what she carried?

Eoin let her move passed him without answering. Her shoulder brushed his chest, and her hip rubbed his thigh, they were so close. Both spots tingled; made him want more.

He turned; wasn't going to allow her to leave him. He looked down, admiring how the denim jeans hugged her bottom and thighs—much an improvement over female attire of his time, which hid such gems from view.

Resting his hand at the small of her back, he guided her through the crowd. A bolt of energy shot up his arm upon first touch, and his mouth went dry. Eoin had the odd wish he was caressing her bare skin.

The lass jumped, as if she'd felt it too, but didn't shake his hand off.

That pleased him but notched his temptation higher. He followed her outside, wanting to move closer, touch more of her than the soft fabric of her shirt.

When the heavy wood door of the pub swung closed behind them, she whirled on him, breaking their physical contact.

"What do you want?" the lass demanded.

How to answer her?

Eoin could ask about the Flag; demand she return it, but the direct approach had rarely worked in the past. Perhaps he could buy it from her?

He was curious as to how she'd acquired it in the first place.

"What're ye called?" he asked instead. He could ease into negotiations so it would be pleasant for both of them.

The lass blinked and her delicate eyebrows drew tight all over again. "Why?"

"Of a suspicious sort, dinnae?" He felt himself smiling; couldn't help it.

"Wouldn't *you* be if a stranger towered over you in a pub? Not to mention followed you outside and won't tell you why."

"Perhaps."

She had a point, but she was a beautiful lass, so wasn't she used to male attention?

Somehow that idea bothered Eoin and he wanted to growl. "I apologize if I startled ye." He reached for his manners and bowed at the waist.

Her eyes went wide, but the pink cheeks charmed him even more.

She let her satchel fall to her side, revealing the front of her form-fitting shirt. It had words on it he didn't try to read, but only because he couldn't look away from the outline of her breasts.

The material wasn't as tight as his, but he could sense the size of the perfect globes. Not huge, but not small, and definitely worth exploring.

Eoin cleared his throat and made himself look back at her bonnie face. "I needed ta talk ta ye, is all."

"About what?" Now she slid the bag behind her, still as if she had to protect it.

Could she know about the Flag?

Maybe he should be direct, after all. Eoin smiled again, wanting to put her at ease. Wanted to touch her too, but instinct told him it'd make her retreat, and that was the last thing he wanted. It wasn't wholly due to the Faery Flag, either.

The lass had enchanted him.

Eoin took a step forward and she took a step back, until her shoulders touched the stone side of the building.

Her eyes went even wider.

"Lass, I dinnae mean ye harm."

She stared for a few moments, then nodded and

relaxed slightly, but didn't separate her body from the building. "I know. I don't know *how* I know, but I do. What do you need to talk to me about?"

Her brown gaze was still more leery than he would've liked, but he could sense curiosity there, too. That could work to his favor.

He took a breath. "I am Eoin MacLeod, an' I fear ye have somethin' tha' belongs ta me."

chapter five

She almost dropped her bag. Who was crazier, her or the man whose earnest sapphire eyes were studying her?

Ashlyn tugged her favorite carry-all back up to her chest and pinned it with both arms. If he advanced on her again, at least she could keep him from getting close. Sorta.

Worries flitted that she'd harm the painting, but she pushed them all away. Needed to protect herself from this huge man if necessary.

The fact that he was hot shouldn't soften her instincts, right?

What'd happened to being sure he wouldn't hurt her?

She'd believed it even before he'd said it.

Ashlyn wanted to take another step back, but the pub wall was still touching her shoulders. She had nowhere else to retreat. "Wh-wh-wh-what?" The stutter fell out and she cleared her throat. "What did you just say?" This was a demand. She spread her feet apart, bracing herself against the stone behind her.

His face softened and he raised an outstretched palm. "Lass, I mean ye no harm, as I've already tol' ye."

The brogue rolled over her, but she did her best to ignore the warmth that curled in her lower belly. This guy could be a crazy Scottish killer, and she was attracted to him?

Idiot.

"What did you say your name was?" Ashlyn barked.

This has to be a sick joke.

Or she was dreaming.

Yes, maybe that's it?

Had she gotten drunk and passed out?

She was really in her bed at the cottage. She'd never had much tolerance for alcohol, and Scottish beer was strong. Kate had insisted she come to the pub…maybe…

Ashlyn had been so curious about Eoin MacLeod she'd dreamt him up, in contemporary clothing and everything?

Then what does his claim about me having something belonging to him mean?

Was he talking about his painting?

In dreamland, that'd totally make sense.

"That's it," she whispered.

"What, lass?" He hadn't answered her demand about his name, but she couldn't tell if he was ignoring her.

"I'm dreaming. I have to be!"

His dark brow furrowed, and he cocked his head

to one side. "Lass?"

Ashlyn pushed off the wall and advanced on him.

He didn't move; let her crowd him, as much as she could anyway, since he was so big.

"I'm dreaming. This isn't real. You can't be Eoin MacLeod." She gestured to his handsome face. "He lived three hundred years ago, so you can't be him. It's just not possible."

The man reared back but didn't move his lower body. They were only about a foot apart now. "Ye know a' me, lass?"

"You? No." She shook her head. "Obviously, you're not paying attention." Ashlyn pointed to him again, then indicated herself. "This is my doing, somehow —"

He grabbed her wrist to still her movements and his gaze bored into hers. "I *am* Eoin MacLeod."

"No..." She shook her head and stared at his mouth.

His grip on her was firm, but gentle; he wasn't hurting her. His scent enveloped her, making her want to expand her lungs more.

Sandalwood and sage; just like one of my books. Better than any cologne.

She wanted to close her eyes but didn't dare look away from the laird doppelgänger. "This is crazy," Ashlyn whispered. She had to pant to breathe. Her face warmed. Her heart slid into overdrive.

What's happening to me?

Was the dream taking a sexy turn?

She'd been intrigued by the painting, so it made sense. Ashlyn had wondered what it would be like to kiss Eoin MacLeod all day, especially after she'd written her new character kissing her heroine.

Her dream was filling in the blanks.

Yes.

He was staring just as hard, and his massive chest heaved as if he was in need of oxygen, too. Like she was affecting him somehow. His eyes slid to her lips.

Ashlyn pushed her tongue out to moisten them and...

Did he just groan?

She gave into the temptation and tilted her face up.

He was probably a foot taller than her five-foot-five inches, so he'd have to dip down to her.

Dream-Eoin didn't disappoint. His lips brushed hers with the barest touch—a question, but it wasn't enough.

Ashlyn pressed forward, into him, against those hard muscles. He probed at the seam of her mouth, and she let him in, whimpering when his tongue rubbed hers.

She dropped her bag and put her arms around his waist. Dream-Eoin pulled her to him, putting his hands on her back and pressing harder into their kiss.

The heat of his palms chased tremors down her spine, and she couldn't help but feel claimed—just from the sheer size of his touch.

The kiss went on until desire threatened to swallow her whole. Heat suffused her whole body, starting in her chest and spreading down her limbs. Ashlyn's legs wobbled and it was a good thing he was holding her up.

Something long and hard pressed into the soft part of her belly, and she pushed closer, her core throbbing an answer, a demand.

Ashlyn had to hand it to herself—and her imagination. This kiss was just as good as the ones she always described in her books. She'd probably wake up horny—

"Ashlyn?"

Someone familiar, female, but she resisted the pull of distraction, and continued to kiss Dream-Eoin.

He groaned again and held her tighter, as if he battled the interruption, too.

"Damn, that *is* you. Go, Ash!"

With a curse, Dream-Eoin tugged his mouth off hers and whirled his body away, pushing Ashlyn behind him as if he needed to protect her. He planted a hand on her hip, keeping her close.

She had to blink a few times to clear her vision and the haze of passion. Hadn't wanted the kiss to end, dammit. Wanted more than just his mouth moving over hers, too. So did her body. If it could scream aloud in protest, it did.

Ashlyn peered around Dream-Eoin's massive arm

and glared at her best friend.

Kate was openly perusing the tall man, then she looked back at Ashlyn. Their gazes locked. "Who's your friend, Ash?" She grinned.

Dream-Eoin looked at her, then back at Kate.

Her bestie was wearing the same hot-to-trot red and black outfit she'd donned to go to the pub, complete with her matching Louies. Her normally impeccable tight ponytail was mussed; fiery strands had escaped and framed her face. Her cheeks were flushed pink, and her mouth swollen, like she'd just been—

Ashlyn gasped.

The bartender.

Her gaze pinballed from Kate to *Not-So*-Dream-Eoin.

Heat seared her cheeks, but it sure as hell wasn't from the arousal she was still coming down from.

She hadn't been dreaming?

Shit.

The other option was crazy, wasn't it?

Ashlyn had let a *stranger* kiss her.

A stranger who'd curled her toes and set her on fire from the inside out.

A stranger that…was a dead ringer for her three-hundred-year-old painting, *and* claimed his name was the same as the long-dead laird's?

Eoin looked at the fulsome redhead who'd joined them outside the pub, then back at the lass he *most certainly* shouldn't have kissed.

What in five hells had come over him?

He blinked and tried to tamp down his arousal. The trews were restricting the blood flow to his tender parts, and he wanted to shift in his boots. The denim also did a poor job of hiding his condition, he suspected. Another reason he should be wearing his plaid.

Embarrassment wasn't a familiar emotion, and he had no need to be introduced today, lest the reason be a third party noticing his erection.

His hand slid from the honey-haired lass' hip, since the other woman wasn't a danger to either of them.

Eoin regretted breaking their physical contact. Wanted to reach for her again, but she'd slid beside him, instead of behind, and he suspicioned she wouldn't appreciate his touch.

Her pretty cheeks were flushed with color, and her hair mussed from where his hands had been in it. Her inviting mouth was swollen from his, and Eoin had to swallow. He wanted her with an intensity he'd not experienced before.

Ashlyn, the other woman had called his lass.

Your lass?

Nay, it wasn't true — and it was foolish.

What had she done to enthrall him so?

Perhaps Korinna wasn't the only witch he was acquainted with.

"Ashlyn?" Eoin asked, liking how her name rolled off his tongue.

Her eyes went as wide as saucers, and she grabbed her giant satchel off the ground beside her, plastering it to her lovely breasts again, with both arms wrapped around it.

He licked his lips, still tasting her there, which just wreaked more havoc on his libido. His cock twitched. The lass had tasted like summer berries and sweet ale, and even now, left him wanting more. He cleared his throat. Eoin didn't lose control—ever.

He had a mission.

She had the Faery Flag.

He couldn't allow ill-timed desire to be an insurmountable obstacle.

His duty wouldn't be thwarted.

Eoin studied her grip on the colorful bag. Her chest was hidden, but he'd felt the weight of her breasts against him, and they were indeed as perfect as he'd suspected. One more moment and he would've cupped them through her shirt—or perhaps under it.

Too bad they'd been interrupted.

He shot a look at the culprit, who was still looking at his Ashlyn, then back at him with narrowed eyes— the sure sign of female ire.

"What *exactly* is going on here?" the lass asked. Her inflection told him she was American like Ashlyn.

She perched a hand on a hip and tilted her head to one side, making her flame-like hair dance.

She was much more Eoin's type, with her endless curves and voluptuous breasts. Especially since her shirt was tight and propped them high, for the visual devouring. She was taller than Ashlyn, too, but he preferred the golden-haired beauty who was scooting away from him by the second.

Regret that had nothing to do with the clan treasure he hunted settled low in his gut. Eoin didn't want her to fear him. He wanted to tug her to his side and comfort her. Kiss her again. Take her. Hold her afterward, too—which was a foreign concept. He *never* coddled his lovers.

At any rate, he needed to find out what she knew about him.

How could she know who he was?

Or that he lived three hundred years in the past— from her time, anyway.

"Uh…" Ashlyn shot him a look full of uncertainty, then looked back at the redhead.

"Ash?" She was wary, too, and she pulled Ashlyn to her, as if she intended to protect her from him. "Is something wrong?"

"No, of course not." His lass gave him another sideways glance and looked back at her friend. "Let's…let's…go back to the cottage, it's late and we're going to Skye early tomorrow." The more she spoke, the more confident her tone became. She'd regained her composure.

Eoin perked up.

Skye?

They were going to his isle?

The fulsome lass threw him another look—this one of derision. "What did you do to my friend?"

"Nothin'," he said. Straightened his shoulders when her pretty face sported a glower. If a look could slay, he would've been on the ground, bleeding out.

Ashlyn tugged her arm. "I'm good, Kate. I just wanna go."

The redhead didn't move right away, until his petite beauty looped her arm inside her elbow and pulled hard enough to dislodge the taller lass' balance.

Eoin didn't move. He wasn't panicked he'd lose the lass—or the Flag. He had magic on his side and now knowledge—she was headed to where his home, Dunvegan, still stood.

He could grab her and *blink* back to the isle right now, with her satchel. His magic was certain the Flag lay within its confines.

It—and *she*—could be his for the taking.

Should he do it, or be reasonable and try to speak with her regarding his clan's property?

Eoin could take the morrow to speak with her.

Following her to Skye wouldn't be an issue, and he could easily arrange a meeting, since he'd not let her out of his sight there, either.

He didn't want her kicking and screaming, but he

did want to take her with him.

Back to his time?

Nay.

He couldn't.

He wanted to.

He...would?

Eoin hedged, shifting in his modern boots. His grandfather *had* taught him a spell to induce sleep. If he used it on his lass, it would save Ashlyn the disorientation of time travel, since she didn't have a medallion.

He couldn't let her leave but didn't want her to know that just yet.

chapter six

ashlyn couldn't help looking over her shoulder as she practically dragged Kate away from the pub.

He was still there, staring in their direction.

She wanted to quicken her step.

"Jesus, let go of me, or slow the hell down! I'm not gonna scratch my Louies…or worse, break a heel. Do you have any idea how much these shoes cost?" her bestie grumbled.

"We have to get back."

Kate yanked away and planted her feet on the ground with a stomp that screamed. She crossed her arms over her chest and glared. "Tell me what the heck is going on, Ashlyn!"

She shook her head.

Her friend scowled. "Right. Now."

"He…he…kissed me, all right?"

"Duh. I've got eyes." She rolled them, as if to prove it.

"I didn't…"

Kate blinked. Waited.

Ashlyn had been about to say she hadn't wanted to kiss the laird-lookalike. That would be a lie. She'd just…

Jesus, can you get more pathetic? Did you really think you were dreaming?

So what if it doesn't make sense, right?

"What?" her bestie prompted. "Did he like, rape-kiss you?"

She winced. "Not exactly…"

"Why do you sound so unsure? I know he's tall, but I could take him. I'll kick him in the balls. Do we need to go back?" Kate started to whirl around, but Ashlyn latched on to her arm.

"Just stop. It's fine. Let's go get some sleep."

"Ash?" Her friend studied her face. "What's wrong with you? You're shaking. I'm gonna kill that bastard."

Ashlyn sucked in a breath and met her friend's seafoam eyes. "You didn't notice…"

"Notice what?"

She opened her bag and dug out the little gilt frame. Couldn't look at Eoin MacLeod, but she held it up to Kate.

"Oh. My. God."

Maybe she *had* noticed the resemblance?

"You brought that with you? To the *pub*?"

Well, maybe not.

"Can't you see it?" Ashlyn flipped the painting and looked into the laird's eyes. Pools of sapphire stared out at her but paled in comparison to the real thing.

Oh God. Get over yourself. He can't be the same guy.

"Ash, you're making me worry." Kate's head was cocked to one side, and she wore a frown.

"He looked just like this guy. Even said his name was Eoin MacLeod. Just like…*him*…in the painting." She rushed her words and fought the urge to close her eyes. Shudders threatened to bowl her over. Maybe she'd really lost it. Being a writer had sucked her rational brain into the ether.

Her friend was silent. Then, after seconds that felt like hours, Kate threw her head back and barked a laugh. "We're in Scotland."

"Yeah? And?"

"That's probably a common name here."

"I don't think—"

"Ashlyn." Kate settled her hands on her shoulders and squeezed. "I think you *do* need to sleep. How much did you have to drink?"

Ashlyn frowned. "*One* beer. Stop trying to make me think I'm crazy. They…look just alike. Look at the painting, I mean, really *look*."

Her bestie's gaze only stayed on the laird for a few seconds before her eyes landed back on Ashlyn's. Classic Kate, when she'd made up her mind and was about to disregard what someone else thought. "Well, they have the same name. Maybe your kissing bandit is a descendant of this guy. Who knows? Scotland's not that big."

"But, Kate—"

"Honey—"

"Don't patronize me, Kathryn Marie Farmer."

She giggled. "Uh oh, you're breaking out the full name?"

Ashlyn glared. "Bite me." She looked toward the pub, but Not-So-Dream-Eoin was gone. However, she couldn't shake the feeling that he *watched* them from somewhere. Another shudder wracked her frame, and she fought the resulting quivers.

His mouth moving over hers had lit her up from the inside. She'd never reacted to a single kiss like that before. She could taste him still; all she had to do was run her tongue along her lips. He'd smelled so good, like naturally, not like a man who used fancy colognes.

Being in his arms, against that massive chest, she'd felt...protected, even if it was cheesy, like what she'd write in one of her books. Ashlyn hadn't had a care in the world—except his mouth taking hers. His tongue against hers. Feeling his erection against her stomach, and the heat in her sex.

She had to squeeze her thighs together to ignore the throb even now.

Wished for Not-So-Dream-Eoin.

He was so hot...

Maybe it's that Scottish beer?

"Ash?"

She jumped at her nickname and looked back at Kate. "He's gone," she whispered.

"Good. He was super-hot, but if he forced his

hands—or his mouth—on you, I'll still hunt him down and kick his ass."

Ashlyn smirked. "He didn't force me. I wanted to kiss him."

Confusion darted across Kate's pretty face. "Then, why—"

"Don't worry about it. It's done. Tell me about the bartender. I assume you and he…snogged?"

Her bestie snickered. "We did. He's hot, too. And those muscles. Just wow. They feel as good as they look, and damn…can he kiss. His name's Bruce and I totally plan to see him again before we leave."

Ashlyn looped her arm in Kate's and swung her bag over her shoulder. "C'mon, tell me all about it. Don't leave any details out. Give me story fodder. I'll write a scene inspired by you!"

Kate grinned and they started to walk to the cottages their tour group was staying at.

Someone—Not-So-Dream-Eoin probably—really was watching them the whole way. She could still feel it. She didn't fear him. It was more…anticipation, as if he'd be Romeo, calling out to her like Juliet, on the tower after they'd kissed the first time.

Oh, hell. That was a tragedy. You realllllly need to get over yourself.

Then again, *tragedy* was pretty apropos for how her interaction with the hot Scot had gone. No matter how good the kiss had been.

Maybe Kate was right. *This* Eoin MacLeod was

simply related to the laird from the 1700s in her painting. The doppelgänger thing could be explained, right? Familial DNA reoccurring three hundred years later?

That has to be it.

Then why…

The way he'd insisted he was Eoin MacLeod, and asked how she knew *'of'* him? His brogue and his word choice were…old school. With a capital O. He'd called her *'lass'*…

Ashlyn shook her head and pushed away the impossible. She focused on Kate's interaction with Bruce and smiled at how her bestie's eyes lit up.

The girl had a serious crush, and it was too bad she'd have to leave the dude behind when they headed home at the end of the week.

It was sad, and the hopeless romantic in her wanted more for her fashion designer friend. Despite what Kate claimed about being busy, and preferring the single life, she deserved love.

They made it to their temporary home after a brisk walk and the naughty story. Her friend opened things up.

Before they could go inside, Ashlyn felt dizzy. Her step faltered and Kate grabbed her arm, but her bestie wavered in her Louies, too, and Ashlyn gripped both her wrists.

They locked eyes and Kate yawned.

"I don't feel right," they said at the same time.

Ashlyn swallowed a yawn of her own, but then the world went black.

Eoin caught both women — barely. He lowered his Ashlyn to the ground as gently as he could, leaning her against the stone cottage's outside wall. He hefted her friend in his arms and toed the door open, entering the small building. It was dark and he didn't feel much like searching for the switch on the wall that would artificially light the place.

Electricity had awed and petrified him the first time he'd encountered it, but wonder had won out, and it was one of the things he wished for in his century.

Korinna had given him a rudimentary lesson of how it worked — which only served to make him even more envious.

Eoin set the lass down on the first bed he came to, praying his spell would keep her asleep for hours — or the whole night. It wouldn't matter for him and Ashlyn — they'd go back to 1755 — but when Kate awoke, she'd find her friend missing and would probably remember everything up to the moment he'd knocked them both out.

There were spells to scramble memories, but he didn't want to make things even worse for her. He wished Ashlyn would've been alone.

He'd been stealthy in his approach and neither

lass had spotted him, so his appearance wouldn't feature in Kate's memories. The redheaded beauty would likely go to the police—another thing his century didn't offer.

They wouldn't be there for the aftermath, but if he returned his lass to the twenty-first century, he could take her right back to this moment, where it would seem as if she'd never left. Aye, it would change history, but it would be for Ashlyn and Kate's benefit, as well as his own. A small ripple in time shouldn't damage much.

If?

Eoin wouldn't have a choice but to return her home. He'd get the Flag and their need to be together would end.

Right?

He growled at his instant rejection of the idea of letting her go.

They didn't know each other.

It was the right thing to do.

Hell, the *right thing* to do was get the Flag *now*, and place Ashlyn on the other bed in the cottage.

Walk away.

Eoin should do just that; like he was leaving the small place now. He could go free and clear; she most likely wouldn't have a clue what'd happened.

He stared down at her beautiful face, still in a repose he'd induced, and a fierce protectiveness rose in his chest, one he'd previously reserved for his sister alone. Naturally, he didn't want to claim Fiona like he did the sleeping lass before him.

Eoin wanted Ashlyn for his own — for keeps.

He didn't even know her surname or her background. She was American, so her people could've come from anywhere. She probably wasn't even Scottish.

Cursing under his breath, he reached for her satchel instead of gathering her to him like he wanted. His magic throbbed; the Flag called.

Lettering caught his attention before he could dive inside. '*Ashlyn George*,' was sewn into the side of the bag, prominent amongst the colorful splotches, in a glistening gold thread.

"George." Like the king he'd begrudgingly sworn fealty to. So many of his countrymen fought the Sassenachs even now. He'd done what he'd had to do to keep his clan, his sister, his grandfa, safe. Didn't have to like it. "Bastard Englishman." Hopefully his Ashlyn wasn't a relation.

Eoin opened the bag, but he couldn't see much of the contents. He slid a hand inside and felt around. His magic hummed when his fingers encountered something hard, but it felt embossed, or like carved wood that'd been smoothed of any rough edges.

He pulled what turned out to be a small fancy frame and dropped the satchel. The thing was gold, like the letters on the bag.

His eyes locked onto — well, his own.

Eoin startled.

What in all the levels of Fae Hell?

Ashlyn had a painting of *him*?

He hadn't sat for any such thing, but perhaps he hadn't *yet* — as far as his time was concerned.

Eoin didn't see the Faery Flag, but his magic screamed it was right before his eyes. He flipped the painting over. The frame was thick. Perhaps, the Flag was *inside* it?

Close voices made him jolt and his eyes darted around. He couldn't see anyone, but the conversation was gaining volume by the second. More American accents were coming toward him — them.

He needed to get Ashlyn and go. What would someone think if they rounded the corner and saw her passed out, leaning against the cottage wall? He couldn't chance *anyone* seeing them, even if he could just play things off by claiming his lass had over imbibed.

Eoin slid the painting back in the satchel and closed the cottage door silently. He threw the bag's straps over his shoulder and lifted Ashlyn into his arms.

Even asleep she cuddled into him, as if seeking warmth, and nestled her face against his neck.

A tremor shot down his spine and he had to suck in a breath. She fit against him as if she was made for him.

The thought jarred him even more, but the voices

were nearer still, so Eoin ordered his feet to move.

Ashlyn was going to have a thing or two to say when she awoke, no doubt, but he'd feel better if they were on 1755 Skye, and out of the twenty-first century.

At least then she couldn't run from him.

chapter seven

Eoin was reluctant to set Ashlyn on the loamy cave floor, even if he had to so he could strip down and open the portal to his time. The Faery Stones required *both* his hands, and the ordered pattern of touch and tone had to be just right.

He quickly undressed, folding his denim trews and the blue shirt. His medallion swayed back and forth as he shoved the garments into his satchel and placed it back in the hiding place. He slipped out of his modern boots and did the same.

Now naked, he took two handfuls of sandy dirt and showered the rocks over the area, so it didn't look recently cleaned off.

He dug his claymore out and pivoted, trotting over to Ashlyn. Eoin laid his sword next to her and pulled the small painting from her bag. After a onceover, he placed it on her chest. Didn't want to take the time dismantling it right there; he'd do it when they were safely in 1755. He could still feel the Flag's call, so it had to be behind his image; nothing else made sense.

She could wake up at any moment, at worst; she'd sleep 'til the morning, at best.

His medallion would also allow him to stay inside of the cave when they arrived back in his time; otherwise, a person was ejected and landed on the beach, a built-in magical protection of the Stones. Unfortunately, the piece's magic didn't change the fact any items accompanying him had to be in his hands or wouldn't make the jump.

Eoin would have to hold the painting in one hand and Ashlyn in his arms at the same time, since she was unconscious. He'd have to leave his beloved sword. He growled. Looked at Ashlyn, then the claymore.

The lass or the sword?

He could come back for it later. He *would*. It was his favorite weapon, despite the others in the armory at Dunvegan.

Eoin darted to the Faery Stones, which awoke with the first brush of his fingers. All five crystals lit up from the inside, and power coursed through him, making his limbs hum. Bouncing on the balls of his bare feet, he hummed to the tone each Stone gave off. He didn't have to chant a spell; the melody was in his blood, and the Stones responded to him without much effort.

He'd always heard the song they played. The Faery Stones had called to him from the time he'd been a wee lad, although he'd not understood the call just then. The only magic stronger was his link to the Flag.

Eoin repeated the pattern, picking up tempo with each touch. The warmth in his body increased but it didn't hurt. It was like the best embrace and left him needing more. Energy pulsed in his temples; making him want to go farther, feel more.

The first *pop* sounded, indicating the portal would open soon. Then the sound of tearing parchment. The following *pop-pop-pop* was each louder than the last, and a magic-born gale swirled around him, making his hair fly in his eyes.

It made Ashlyn's golden locks dance around her shoulders, too, but she remained oblivious, in a deep sleep despite the wind throwing sand around her.

Magic worked up so much heat inside him, the moving air was like a caress, offering blissful coolness to Eoin's exposed skin.

It felt good. Better than good. A relief.

White light shot straight up to the cave's ceiling from the center crystal of the Faery Stones, the last step before the portal's birth.

Anticipation hit him in waves, making his gut clench, and he released his hold on the final crystal. Eoin darted to his lass and gathered her to him but held her upright against his chest instead of prone in his arms. He plastered one hand to the small of her back and gripped the gilt frame in the other.

She was light as a feather, so he could hold her with no issue. He only had to step forward a few paces to be through the portal when it opened anyway.

Eagerness and urgency fluttered in his stomach. He wanted to be home. With this lass. In his arms…in his bed.

Eoin ordered himself to calm. He felt like he was fleeing, doing something wrong. He banished the instant *you are!* floating around in his head.

He was taking Ashlyn to his time against her will.

The existence of magic, let alone walking through centuries, would be a shock to her.

An iridescent orb appeared before them, distracting him. He'd have no choice but to reveal everything, but that was for later. They still had to get home.

The whole cavern shimmered and wavered as the glowing bubble grew. It hovered above the ground before floating downward, stopping a few inches in the air. At first hazy, opaque, it started to clear, like multicolored clouds retreating. It got larger and larger by the second, until a sandy floor was visible, and a dimness that was backlit by the Stones in his time.

A mirror image of where Eoin was now, except it was three hundred years in the past. Korinna's magic helped keep his time travel private, in a way, since the Stones let him remain inside the cave.

He hefted Ashlyn higher and stepped up to the portal, making sure his grip was steady on the painting. His medallion lit up, glowing blue, and heating his chest where it lay. A colored aura brightened his lass' face, and he studied each freckle on her gorgeous cheekbones.

Seconds passed that felt like hours as he entered

the bubble.

His heart raced with the sense of nothingness that always washed over him, through him. Eoin couldn't feel anything, even his Ashlyn in his arms, although he could see her. He couldn't feel the painting in his hand, either, and fought the rising panic.

Rationally, Eoin knew all was well, and the disorientation wouldn't last long, thanks to the magic orb hanging from his neck. He couldn't see anything in front of him, but it too would recede in seconds.

His feet touched sand again and he breathed a sigh of relief, shifting the lass in his arms. The portal snapped shut with a *pop*, but the Faery Stones of his time were still lit, dimly illuminating the cave.

He studied Ashlyn to make sure nothing was amiss; she was still well and whole against him, but awareness shot down his spine.

She was as naked as he, and still plastered to his chest.

Eoin swallowed as his cock jumped. Their kiss outside the pub teased his mind. He could remember her taste even now and…God's blood, he wanted more.

She's asleep, you beast.

The little touch of conscience didn't keep him from lowering his mouth to claim hers.

When she moaned and opened for him, warnings went off in his head, but Eoin deepened their kiss, rubbing his tongue against hers.

He dropped the painting to the sand and caressed her soft back, following the curve of her bottom. Ashlyn's breasts were flush to him and felt just as he'd imagined. He wanted to lay her down and explore every inch of her skin. Eoin would have to wait to study her naked body, because he was too eager, but he would...and worship her.

Taste her, touch her, take her.

His arousal was pinned between their bodies, and he was getting harder by the second, by the stroke of her tongue against his.

"Lass." Eoin pushed the word into her mouth. "Jesu, how I wan' ye."

Ashlyn's lips stopped moving and she stilled in his grip before breaking the seal of their mouths. Her pretty brown eyes went from heavy-lidded and hazy with desire, to so wide they bared the whites, in less than a heartbeat. She put her palms to his chest and pushed back, making distance between them Eoin didn't want to allow.

When she lowered her lashes, glancing down, her cheeks went crimson up to her ears, and a gasp fell from her lips. She looked around the cave and swallowed. Ashlyn put force behind her touch and tugged against his hold.

Reluctantly Eoin released her, then regretted the break of their physical contact, and made a go for her, but his lass slid back on her heels.

He should say something — anything — but words

refused to be born.

Confusion darted across her beautiful face when she took another look-see, and then Ashlyn's eyes ran up and down his form, no doubt taking in his nudity. Her face got even redder, making her delicious freckles prominent.

The dirty scoundrel he was couldn't help but look over her bare form, either.

Her breasts were high and tight—neither too large nor too small—as suspected when clothed. Her dusky nipples were peaked, as if his lass had enjoyed their kiss, after all.

Like the first time Eoin had kissed her.

His gaze went lower, studying the roundness of her bottom, the perfect meld to a flat stomach and shapely hips. The tight sparse curls that guarded her sex made *him* have to swallow hard.

Her legs were long for someone so petite, and he wanted them wrapped around her waist while he plunged inside her.

Ashlyn swallowed again and put her palms high and flat, as if to stave him off. "Please, God, tell me this time I *am* dreaming."

"Nay, lass, ye dinnae be." The brogue rolled over her, like the other times he'd spoken, and she tried to push the *eject* button on her senses.

She crushed her eyes shut. Maybe if she counted

to ten, or knocked her heels together, or some shit, maybe…just maybe, Ashlyn would open her eyes and there wouldn't be a very hot, very *naked* man in front of her.

Wait. Did you really just wish for that?

He was aroused, too, sporting an erection that would make any of her heroes proud—and their heroines happy, provided he knew how to use it. If a man who looked like him didn't…well, that'd be a shame.

What're you thinking? You wanna volunteer to be a judge?

Ashlyn was afraid of the answer, so she didn't continue the internal monologue. Much.

Answering yourself makes you cray cray anyway, right?

Not-So-Dream-Eoin, the laird-lookalike, had kissed her…again.

Right?

Ashlyn had kissed him back, too, and it'd been just as oblivion-inducing as the first time. Then she'd woken in his arms, in her…birthday suit?

Why the *hell* was she naked?

Why was *he*? Although she shouldn't complain. His muscles had muscles, and he was standing before her as un-shy as a guy could get.

Maybe he knew he was hot.

But…but…naked?

It's not a dream? Why can't I remember anything?

Had they agreed to some tryst in a…

"Where are we?" Ashlyn blurted, taking another step back. Her eyes darted to the sandy ground, then shot back up, only to land behind Not-So-Dream-Eoin on…crystals? "What the—"

"We're on Skye. My home."

Right, like that explained everything. Ashlyn was supposed to go to Skye, to tour part of the Clan MacLeod stronghold, Dunvegan.

How does he *factor into that?*

Her clothes weren't anywhere in sight either, but she'd worry about that when he got to the tell-all. She waited for him to continue, but he didn't.

Ashlyn covered her breasts, but that left the more important goody bare. She shot her hand down to conceal her sex, then settled for her arm across her chest.

He smirked, and her face seared.

Yeah, yeah.

He'd already seen it all.

She'd been…in his arms.

Against that…glorious chest.

Naked.

Oh. God.

Ashlyn wanted to slap both her hands over her face, but she resisted the urge in order to umpire her girlie bits.

His muscles felt as good as they looked if memory served. Unfortunately, it did.

Dammit.

"What…is…" She puffed out a breath and straightened her shoulders, but still didn't drop her hands. "Going. On?"

Instead of answering, he started rifling through a hide bag on the ground. He'd pulled it from the corner of the…

"Are we in a cave?" Ashlyn studied the ceiling, which was complete with stalactites. That didn't explain the creepy lit-crystal thingies, which seemed to be perched on top of five stalagmites.

Actually, they looked to be a natural part of it, which was weird. Crystals didn't occur like that. Also, the half-circle was too perfect, like someone had *put* them there. In a specific order. They were lit up and giving off light, that brightened the cave.

How, with a side of what-the-hell?

Not-So-Dream-Eoin straightened and tossed her some ivory fabric.

Her arms rose to catch it on reflex, but at least it hid the front of her body.

"Put that on. 'Twill be big, 'tis mine, but it'll cover ye." He lay down and was in the process of wrapping a plaid she recognized as Clan MacLeod's tartan-pattern around his waist as he spoke. Soon, he rose and belted it on.

Awareness zinged down Ashlyn's spine and danced across her chest, then down her arms as she watched. Her heart tripped.

Not-So-Dream-Eoin in a freaking kilt?

Hotness factor just amplified…by a thousand percent.

She reached for her irritation with both hands and tried to glare. Also, to tamp down her ill-timed libido. Sure, she hadn't gotten laid in a while, but imagining licking every inch of his skin—especially since she'd *just* seen him naked—was *highly* inappropriate.

How was he hotter covered up?

Ashlyn cleared her throat. "Why aren't you answering me?"

He closed the distance between them and tried to take her hand, but she scooted back. Sand burned her heels.

"As much as I'd prefer ye naked, ye should dress." His voice was low and had that rolling-over-her-like-butter effect she was coming to despise.

She whipped the shirt down and in front and glared. "Tell me what's going on."

That sapphire gaze locked onto her breasts.

Ashlyn cursed and fought the urge to close her eyes when her cheeks combusted. She shoved her arm into what she thought was a sleeve, and succeeded in getting tangled, with one arm straight up in the air, trapped inside the shirt, with it over her head.

Dammit, it smelled just like him, too.

Sandalwood and sage. As appealing as he was.

Double dammit.

He chuckled, and it washed over her better than

his brogue.

Heat hugged her form, but she wanted to kill him just the same.

Ashlyn tried to dance away from him—and only ended up slamming into his chest. Embarrassment made her body burn—all over.

She prayed for the ground to open up and swallow her, *right now,* even as warm hands stilled her banshee-like movements.

"Lass, allow me ta help ye."

Ashlyn groaned.

He must've taken that as an assent, because he righted the material and bent her arm like a two-year-old, tenderly, and put it through the correct hole. He did the same with the other when she made no move to fight him. "Ah, my leine looks good on ye." Not-So-Dream-Eoin tied the ties at the neck too, but it didn't help the thing stay up—much.

She couldn't look at him even after the shirt settled over her. It stopped mid-thigh and concealed what it needed to, was comfy, too, if huge. The tunic slipped off her shoulder, but he righted it and patted the flesh he'd just covered.

That was when the waterworks started.

Ashlyn scorned every sniffle, and scorned Not-So-Dream-Eoin when he hooked a finger under her chin and tugged up.

Made her look at him.

"Lass? Why're ye cryin'?" His dark brow was

drawn tight, and those incredible eyes were clouded with concern.

"I don't know!" she wailed and let him gather her to that hard — very bare — chest. Why she was letting a stranger comfort her should've demanded more attention in her brain, but then again, she'd let him kiss her, too.

Twice.

With the first stroke of his hand down her back, Ashlyn was a goner to him anyway. Plastered to his body, pressing as close as she could get. She could feel the heat of his thighs burning hers even through the wool of his kilt. She shivered, but she wasn't cold.

He rubbed over the fabric of his shirt. It was rough against her skin…like it was old school hand-woven material, but it didn't hurt. He murmured something she didn't understand, she suspected Gaelic.

"I'm sorry," he whispered in English, into her hair.

Ashlyn sucked back a half-sob and pulled away to look up at him. "Why?"

"I…took ye."

"What d'you mean?" She frowned.

His Adam's apple bobbed as he swallowed. "I…had ta have ye."

Again, there were no blaring sirens, and there *should* have been. No internal order to get away from him. She wanted to…burrow closer. Ashlyn blinked. "What?" was all she could muster.

Did he mean he'd kidnapped her?

She really should examine that. Then demand more from him.

Immediately.

Gently, he released her and moved away, bending to pick something up off the cave's sandy floor. Gold paint glinted in the light from the crystal-thingies.

"Wait. Is that my painting?"

He wore an appealing smirk when their gazes met. "Well, truth be told, 'tis *my* paintin' but I dinnae sit for it yet."

Ashlyn frowned. "What?"

That doesn't make sense.

She made a go for the frame, but he held it out of her reach. She gasped when he flipped it over and started pulling at the back. "Stop! What're you doing?"

The Scottish hottie ignored her and kept moving his fingers until she heard a sickening crack.

Ashlyn winced. "Don't break it!" This was half-plea; half-order and he spared her a look. She darted forward, wanted to grab his wrist, but was afraid to touch him. "Stop. Please."

"Dinnae fash, lass. Ye'll have my visage returned ta ye shortly, if ye wish it. I need tha Flag."

"What're you talking about? Don't break my picture!" She didn't even care that she just made a really rude demand.

He ignored her, and in about two seconds had the frame removed from the small painting.

The laird-lookalike flashed a triumphant grin that had her insides wobbly.

Not-So-Dream-Eoin held up a battered, silky-looking ivory scrap of material. "I have it!"

"What the heck is that? And why was it with my painting?"

chapter eight

"Where the *hell* do you think you're taking me?" Ashlyn kicked against him, but Eoin held her fast. "Put me down! I can walk, dammit. You can't just pick me up as an answer and carry me off! What're you, some kinda damn barbarian?" She *oomphed* over his shoulder and smacked his back.

He *tsked* and tried not to smile. "That mouth on ye, lass. Ye'd better watch what ye say when we get ta Dunvegan. Nessie dinnae like such, an' 'twill likely wash yer mouth."

She stilled in his grip, and he resisted the urge to feel her bare bottom under his leine.

He'd slung her over his shoulder, and keeping his hands at the back of her knees to hold her steady was a challenge. Eoin wanted to run his fingertips over every inch of her creamy thighs before delving deeper, into the silky folds of her sex.

Unmanly quivers wracked him, and he straightened, shifting her higher. Tried to ignore the jolt that went through his cock. Soon, no amount of readjusting his plaid was going to hide arousal. He needed to get his control back.

"Wait. What?" Ashlyn pounded his bare back with a small fist. "Dunvegan? What're you talking about? You still haven't said a damn thing to me, then you manhandle me? Put. Me. Down."

Eoin sighed. He'd ignored all her queries and demands. He didn't know *what* to tell her. The truth would shoot her ire higher. "Will ye vow no' ta run away?"

She harrumphed. "Where *exactly* am I supposed to go, half-naked?"

Instead of answering, he allowed her to slide down to the ground, hyperaware of her breasts shifting against his chest, rubbing through the material he wanted to rip off. He swallowed and shifted in his deerskin boots.

Her brown eyes burned him, but her face was adorably pink, and she yanked his leine down. "Tell me everything."

He nodded. "As I've tol' ye, my name's Eoin MacLeod. I'm called tha Guardian a' tha Faery Flag. When it changes hands, I must go whenever tha' may be ta get it."

Confusion darted across her gorgeous face. "When? Don't you mean where?"

"Nay. *When.*"

"That doesn't make sense. Besides, the Faery Flag is locked up with the rest of the MacLeod treasures. I was supposed to have a tour of Dunvegan today. I wanted to take a picture of it."

"Ye ken a' my home? My clan?"

She nodded as if distracted and looked around the beach.

The water lapped against the shore behind them. It had a calming effect on him, as it'd always had.

Ashlyn took a few steps away from him, exploring, but Eoin didn't stop her. It was probably foolish to trust her, but he did.

"We're on Skye?"

"Aye. I've brought ye back in time. Ta my time."

She whirled on him; eyes wide. "What?"

"I'm sorry ta tell ye this way, but 'tis tha year of our Lord, seventeen hundred an' fifty-five."

"What?" his Ashlyn shouted and jumped back when he approached.

"Let's venture ta Dunvegan, an' I shall explain everathin'."

"No! Tell me *now*!"

Eoin shook his head, and his hair tickled his neck. "Nay, I want ye ta meet someone, he'll help." His grandfather could put things into perspective with her more than he could.

Ashlyn fought his urgings, so he again swung her over his shoulder, amongst shouts, kicks, and hits. She got a few good ones in, and he winced. His thighs and shoulders would bruise for sure, but he'd get them both back to his home in one piece.

The trek took twice what it should've because of the wiggly lass in his arms, but he didn't want to harm her, or have her get away.

Ashlyn loose in his time could be a real danger. It could get her dead at the hands of bandits. Or raped, due to her attire.

"We've arrived. I'm goin' ta put ye down. Dinnae struggle, lass." Eoin pulled her into his arms and held her for a moment. He couldn't help the chuckle that breeched his lips at the adorable fury on her face, but Ashlyn didn't find it funny.

If anything, her expression tightened even more.

"Behold, Dunvegan." He put her to her feet facing the castle gates, but held her shoulders, and pulled her back into his chest. Wouldn't risk her slipping away.

"What the…what are these gates? Where're the power lines? And the flag on top? I saw it in pictures!" When she looked up at him, her face drained of color. Her freckles stood out, but not with the charming crimson he'd liked so much before.

"Lass—"

"You weren't lying…" Ashlyn repeated the phrase over and over, her shoulders caved in, even though her back was still against his chest.

"Ashlyn."

She jolted when he said her name. "I'm not dreaming?"

Her tone was so hopeful it made his gut clench.

"Nay, lass. I know 'tis a fright ta ye. I had ta bring ye home wit' me."

"My laird, all is well?" One of his many cousins,

Alpin, rounded the gate with his hand on his claymore's hilt.

Seeing the big weapon made Eoin grieve his own. He'd have to go get it soon. None other in the armory would do. "Nay, nay." He gestured for emphasis.

"You have guards?" Ashlyn asked. "My laird?"

He gathered her into his arms, lifted her against his chest, and for once she didn't protest. "Ye will call me Eoin."

She muttered something that sounded like, "Not-So-Dream-Eoin," under her breath, but he didn't understand fully, other than his muffled name, and the word, *dream*.

Eoin was swarmed by Nessie, Peg and the Irish lass they'd taken in as a child, Maegan, when he made it into the great hall.

"Who's tha lass?"

"Is she weel?"

"How can we help, my laird?"

"Wha' happened ta her?"

"Where's her clothin'?"

"Why, she's nearly bare, my laird!"

"Lasses!" He raised his voice. "The lass needs bathed an' clothed. Draw a bath in my room, in my tub."

Nessie, the woman who ran Dunvegan since he'd not yet married, furrowed her graying brow, but he didn't have time to worry about decorum.

He needed Ashlyn warm and dry.

"Do it," Eoin ordered. "I'm goin' ta see Grandfa." He set Ashlyn to her feet and cupped her shoulders, wishing he could caress her bare skin. Somewhere. Anywhere. However, he was very aware of the three sets of eyes watching them. "Lass, I'll be back wit' ye shortly. Bathe. Warm yerself. Nessie 'twill get ye somethin' to wear."

"Proper," the older woman whispered.

Ashlyn wavered on her feet, but she nodded. She appeared dazed. Was still too pallid for his liking.

Not that Eoin blamed her. The shock was *his* fault. He should take her back to her time, but…he couldn't. Not just yet anyway. He tilted her chin up. "Look a' me, lass," he whispered.

She did so, but it was seconds before she focused on him. "Eoin…"

If the household lasses were surprised, she'd addressed him so casually, they hid it well.

"Aye, lass. 'Tis me. Eoin. I'll be back soon. I've need ta speak with my grandfa, then I'll take ye ta him. Go wit' the lasses. They'll take care a' ye."

Ashlyn grabbed his hand when he started to whirl away. "Eoin. Don't…be gone long. Please."

His heart jumped and he had to swallow. Her desperation was a live thing that wrapped around him. *He* was the one in the wrong.

Eoin had taken her from where she belonged in time because he was a selfish sod.

It wasn't right that she'd cling to *him*, even though

he was all she knew here, *and* he liked how it made him feel.

"Dinnae be long a' tall, Ashlyn." He looked at Nessie. "Put her in Fiona's green dress."

"Aye, my laird."

He left the women, even though his body begged him to stay at Ashlyn's side, protect her.

From what? Three lasses of his clan?

One of which, who'd helped raise him?

Eoin shook his head and made his fist knock on the door to his grandfather's rooms.

"Eoin-lad, 'tis ye?"

"Aye, Grandfa, I'm home." He pushed into the room, the scent of peat and sage almost equal parts welcoming and overwhelming washed over him. Familiar. Very much his grandfather's abode.

"Ah, lad. Good ta see ye braw! Did ye find tha Flag?"

"Aye, I've brought it home."

Angus MacLeod chuckled and shook his head, stroking his white beard. "Ye ken that dinnae work, my lad." He stood to his full height from his seat near the lit hearth and stretched his shoulders, his back. He groaned with the movements. "'Twill call ye forward again."

Eoin frowned. "Are ye well?"

His grandfather was old, two and ninety on his last birthday, but his Fae blood kept him agile most of the time, much more so than a normal man of his very advanced age. They didn't know what his lifespan would be, since he was a halfling, the son of a full-blooded Fae. Usually, he had no problems moving around.

"Aye, lad, dinnae fash o'er me." He crossed the room and closed the distance between them, grasping Eoin's forearm. "Is all weel, my laird? Ye dinnae look as if 'tis."

He tried not to sigh.

Whether it magic or paternal intuition, the man always knew when something was bothering him.

Was damn irritating most of the time.

"Nay. Tha Flag is here. Safe." For the sake of distraction, Eoin held up the item of discussion, caressing the silky folds before handing it over to his father's father.

"Ah, feels good ta have magic in my hands again," Angus said softly.

This man had raised him from age thirteen, when his father, Gregor, had been killed in a riding accident. His mother had never gotten over it, and died of a fever some months later, after giving birth to Fiona. His younger sister hadn't known either of their parents.

Eoin had been fostering with the MacKinnon Clan, nearby on the isle, but he'd come home to bury his father and start training to be a laird — as well as honing his magic, something he couldn't get anywhere but at Dunvegan.

His grandmother, Lila, had of course raised them as well, but she'd passed away some ten years ago. He missed her smile and sharp wit. She'd been a healer, a skilled one from the future…like his Ashlyn.

Angus watched him, blue eyes keen, despite the creases in his bearded face. The man stroked his long white whiskers, narrowed his gaze, and cocked his head to one side, making his wild white hair dance. "What're ye keepin' from me, my lad? Dinnae make me pull it ou' a' ye."

Eoin dragged his hand through his long hair and the confession tumbled out. "I've brought someone back wit' me."

A smile cracked his grandfather's wrinkled face. "A lass?"

chapter nine

The women talked so fast it was hard to make out that they were speaking English. Their accents seemed thicker than Eoin's, but one was different, more like a combination of Irish and Scottish, which made the brogue even harder to make out. Then the Gaelic.

When they reverted to their native language, Ashlyn could only stare. The melodious words were almost like singing as they shot sentences back and forth. Even if she'd understood Gaelic, she doubted she would've been able to keep up.

Confusion swirled around in her head. Fascination and horror kept advancing and retreating along with it. More *what the hell* collided with the fact Eoin *hadn't* lied. He'd brought her *back in time*.

Really. It isn't a dream.

Ashlyn was too overwhelmed to protest.

They shuffled her up some stairs and into a large room. A warm fire was already glowing from the hearth and the earthy scent of peat tickled her nose.

She tried to look around, but the dark oversized furniture was a blur as three sets of hands pushed her forward, and the youngest girl—a curvy brunette—

tugged on her hand, a gentle smile on her mouth.

Again, she should be fighting this — them — but she didn't know if she wanted to curl into a ball and sob or run.

Then a few teen boys came in with a large wooden tub and set it near the fire. They came and went a few times with buckets of steaming water until the bathtub was full. Inviting, too, with the steam wafting above the rim.

The older woman with salt and pepper hair in a bun at the back of her neck barked orders, and the boys didn't hesitate to obey. She tested the water and wiped her hands on her off-white apron. Her clothing was dark and looked rough.

No doubt all three women wore wool, heavy, but warm enough for the climate. Durable, too. They probably didn't have many replacement outfits.

Ashlyn should pay attention — since she was surrounded by things she'd written about many times.

And isn't that just surreal?

Soon the door was shut, the boys were gone, and she was alone with the three women.

The girl who'd taken her hand started pulling on Eoin's shirt. "Come now, lass," she whispered. She was the one with the weird combo accent, but her smile was still in place, and genuine.

Her rounded cheeks made her green eyes all that more appealing, and she was pretty. Open, friendly.

Ashlyn didn't mean to resist, but then again, she

didn't have much choice. Plus, she really did want to take a bath.

She lifted her arms when bid by the other younger woman, and in about two seconds she was naked by the tub.

The eldest woman urged her to step into the water. "Alls well, lass." She smiled, too, then addressed the third girl, who had reddish-brown hair, and wore a dress almost the same color. "Go fetch tha gown tha laird wanted tha lass in. She looks ta be of a size wit' Lady Fiona, so gather underclothes as well. Our lady dinnae mind."

The girl nodded and was off, closing the door a lot quieter than the last boy had.

Ashlyn shivered, despite the warm fire not ten feet from her and the hot water she was about to get into. Her surroundings hadn't really sunk in—the century she was in—so she was like a prairie dog on alert. She faded from *this is reality* to *no way*, in a circle. "Lady Fiona?" Her voice sounded shaky to her own ears.

"Tha laird's younger sister. 'Tis a delight, tha' one." The older woman's smile widened. Her obvious affection for Eoin's sister warmed Ashlyn somehow.

She felt safe for the first time since being rushed inside Dunvegan, version 1755. Maybe the manhandling didn't bother her so much, either. At least for the moment.

"Go on, lass, inta the tub. We need ye warm," the

other girl said. "I'm Maegan, by tha way." She grinned, and it had a mischievous edge.

"I'm Nessie." The older woman's expression softened. "Tha one I sent off is Peg. These are a few of my lasses."

Ashlyn sank into the hot water with a sigh, resting her back against the fabric-covered wooden side. She bent her knees, but it didn't matter, both women had already seen her naked. The water surrounded her body, almost too warm, but it felt like a caress, increasing her sense of security in a way. Making her just a touch more comfortable with her very odd— unbelievable—situation.

They fussed over her, washing her hair with a flowery scented soap, but she was grateful for feeling clean again. Soap like that was probably a luxury for them, so Ashlyn appreciated it, even if she couldn't tell them.

The two women washed her body as if she was a child and wouldn't accept her attempt at, "I can do it myself," so she let them do their thing. It felt good, anyway.

She couldn't help but think of Eoin's hands all over her in that cave. Then his mouth moving over hers, even if it was the second time, she'd not *really* wanted to kiss him.

Right?

Her cheeks burned, and she avoided their gazes, even though there was no way they were mind readers.

When either spoke, it was mostly to each other, not asking much of Ashlyn—although she'd kind of expected the opposite. For instance, "Why were you with our laird, nearly naked?" led the charge in her head, but nothing of the sort was mentioned.

Maybe they knew better than to question Eoin—or her, as an extension of that, but they'd all made multiple inquiries when they'd been down in the great hall.

The laird had ignored them, so maybe that was it.

The door creaked as it opened and Peg was back, but she wasn't alone. An ebony-haired girl, who had to be in her late teens was on her heels, and both females had armfuls of fabric.

Ah, the eighteenth-century feminine attire.

They were going to truss Ashlyn up.

Oh my God. This is real.

No amount of repeating the idea alleviated her *oh shit.* She swallowed and sat taller in the tub.

The new girl's gaze glued to Ashlyn's and her heart skipped.

Curiosity was etched in the eyes that matched Eoin's.

She had to be his sister. Ashlyn could see him in her face, as well. The sibling resemblance was clear in the high cheekbones and the shape of their eyes.

She was gorgeous, with natural alabaster skin Kate would be jealous as hell of. Her beauty stunned

Ashlyn—not unlike the redhead who owned the shop she'd bought Eoin's painting at.

"Hello," she croaked, then yelled at herself.

"Good day," the girl returned. She set her burden down on a trunk at the end of the four-poster bed and curtseyed. Her smile was wide, and she had a dimple in her right cheek.

The other servant—Peg—started straightening the garments out.

"I'm Fiona," the dark-haired beauty said.

"My name's Ashlyn," she whispered as Nessie urged her to stand and step out of the tub onto some sort of animal fur rug. The hairy texture teased her toes, and she fidgeted. She was naked in front of four people now, with nowhere to hide.

Maegan wrapped her in a sheet of material—a towel eighteenth century style. It wasn't very soft, but it got the job done as the girl started rubbing down Ashlyn's arms and back.

Kate wouldn't approve. Bath towels were supposed to be lavish, thick and soft.

The second thought of her bestie jolted her in her skin.

Her head spun. Ashlyn was really *here*.

Back…in time. In the past.

Like she'd stepped into one of her stories.

She wavered on her feet, and her arms were contained in the linen, so she couldn't even reach out to steady herself.

No amount of squeezing her eyes shut and shouting *no, no no, please no!* in her head was working. Dizziness swamped her, and Ashlyn swayed.

She wanted Eoin.

Why? He kidnapped you, idiot!

"She's gonna fall," Peg warned.

Hands seized her shoulders before Ashlyn could tell them she was fine.

Was she?

No. Not even an iota of 'okay.' Not even close.

Fiona's pretty face was marred with a frown. "Are ye well, lass? Ashlyn, ye said?" The girl struggled with her name—it wasn't period appropriate, after all.

"I'm…I'm…I don't know!" She tried not to wail, but damn tears blurred her vision again. They were hot on her cheeks, too, and she couldn't muster the energy to wipe them away.

Four sets of eyes watched her with concern, and the MacLeod women wore nearly identical frowns and furrowed brows.

"Shit," Ashlyn whispered. She shook her head.

Nessie gasped.

The other two servants exchanged nervous looks, but amusement rippled Eoin's little sister's full mouth.

"I like her," the girl announced.

The older woman muttered something in Gaelic and *tsked.* Her lips were pursed, and she crossed her arms over her ample breasts.

Ashlyn's cheeks seared. Eoin had said the older

woman didn't like cursing, so she *should* watch her mouth.

Kate wouldn't be able to cut it here, her favorite word started with an *f* and ended with a *k*.

Ashlyn avoided Nessie's gaze and looked at Eoin's little sister. "I guess that's good," she said.

Fiona flashed her dimple and grabbed what had to be a chemise from the end of the bed. "Let's get ye dressed."

"The laird said he'd be back fer her," Maegan said.

"He's wit' Grandfa, tha' could take hours." Fiona rolled her eyes.

Peg took the chemise and tugged it over Ashlyn's head. The material was butter-soft, and she palmed it as it settled over her body. It was lower cut than it'd appeared to be when Fiona had handled it, but she wasn't surprised it would only be the first of multiple layers.

Ashlyn wasn't looking forward to the corseted top on the green gown. Her breasts weren't huge, but they were too large to go without some sort of support.

Unlike Kate, who wore corsets for fun, she wasn't a fan.

"That's so pretty," she blurted when Fiona lifted the shimmery material and held it up.

It was a lighter color than it'd appeared when lying flat, a Kelly Green, with an intricate pattern of leaves embroidered into the bodice and at the bottom of the skirt in a darker green thread that caught the light as it moved.

The teen beamed. "'Tis mine, an' I fancy it verra much."

"Thank you for letting me wear it."

"Oh, 'tis no bother." She frowned. "My brother dinnae approve a' it."

"Oh."

Nessie urged Ashlyn to turn toward the fire as they got the yards and yards of fine fabric over her head.

The gown rustled as it fell into place, and Ashlyn had to resist caressing the elaborate embroidery. When she looked down, it hit her *why* Eoin wouldn't want his baby sister wearing the thing. It was so low cut, if she bent over, she feared her boobs would pull a Janet Jackson.

Heat washed over her body, burning up to her ears. The crimson flush was visible on the bare skin of her chest, too. Ashlyn wanted to cover up, and she wasn't even with *him* yet.

How would Eoin feel about *her* in this gown?

Then again, he'd seen her naked, too.

It was fine, no doubt expensive for the time, true lady's attire. Kate would love it for her fantasy collection.

They made quick work of the ties at the back, but thankfully Peg and Maegan didn't pull the corset so tight Ashlyn couldn't breathe.

However, her breasts were on display. She was

rocking cleavage that would make her bestie proud. She gulped.

Fiona clapped. "So bonnie, Ashlyn!"

"Tha lass does tha' gown well." Nessie's pride was obvious and made her want to fidget.

Peg and Maegan beamed, taking turns going on about how lovely she was.

They made quick work of her hair, putting it up in what Ashlyn considered close to a French twist.

A part of her was giddy, like she was going to a ball, and another part was terrified, and couldn't help the shudders that threatened, shaking her to her core. She was dressed up like a lady, like she was going to some Renn Fest, but this was *real*.

She was in 1755, and this *wasn't* a dream.

Could this trip be the most authentic research she ever did?

Ashlyn snorted.

Guess that's thinking positive, right?

"Come ta my rooms! I've a lookin' glass!" Fiona tugged her hand.

"Slow down, milady. The laird will require Lady Ashlyn's presence," Nessie admonished.

Lady Ashlyn?

"Wait. I'm not—"

"I'll take her ta them!" the girl exclaimed, obviously not daunted by the older woman.

Fiona pulled her from the room in a blur and dragged her down a long hallway.

Ashlyn wanted to look around, but the girl had them at top speed and it was all she could do to keep up.

Eoin's sister's room had an obvious feminine touch the room they'd been in had lacked, from the padded window seat to the slender carved pillars on the bed. There was a large MacLeod tartan covering the bedding, but under it was a fur blanket that made Ashlyn want to curl up against it to see if it was as soft as it looked.

The room was warmer, because it was smaller, and the fire burned bright.

The teen went to the corner immediately, leaving Ashlyn by the bed, and dragged an intricately carved, harp-shaped mirror over by the fireplace. Fiona beckoned. "Come, Lady Ashlyn."

"You don't have to call me that. I'm not a lady."

"Ah, but ye look like one."

Her eyes found themselves in the cloudy reflection, and they went wide with the shock Ashlyn could see all over her face. "Holy shit," she whispered.

Fiona giggled. "Dinnae my brother tell ye? Dinnae speak as such around Nessie."

Heat flared all over, and she locked eyes with the girl's deep blue ones. "Uh. Sorry."

Eoin's sister grinned. "Dinnae bother me. But Grandfa is also…sensitive ta curses. From a lass, anaway."

"Good to know. Thanks." Ashlyn smiled.

"Ye...speak...unusual." The girl frowned. Her black hair was long, hanging loose in thick waves to her waist, and shifted as she cocked her head to one side. Her gown was rich fabric, like the green one, but it had a modest neckline and was deep red. It also had pink flowers embroidered on the bodice.

Fiona was definitely a girly girl. Kate would approve.

"Ah. I'm not...from around here." She didn't want to pull the whole *I'm-from-the-future* thing until she talked to Eoin. Ashlyn swallowed. Averted her eyes back to her reflection.

The gown was probably the finest thing she'd ever worn. She wanted to twirl.

Fiona was still studying her—she could sense it from her peripheral vision, but the laird's little sister didn't make further inquiries.

Maybe Eoin had everyone trained?

"Come, I'll take ye ta my Grandfa's chambers. Ne'er good ta keep my brother waitin'."

Ashlyn didn't argue, but her heart jumped at the thought of seeing Eoin again.

chapter ten

Shuffling feet and a soft knock at the door made Eoin look up.

"Come," his grandfather called.

The familiar dark head of his little pest peeked in, and his instinct was to yell at her to return to her rooms—or demand to know why she was defying his orders—but Fiona wasn't alone.

Eoin blinked at the flash of green fabric.

Ashlyn stepped into the room and stood beside his younger sister. She fidgeted at Fiona's side, her discomfort a live thing he could feel, like her desperation, had been earlier in the great hall.

It didn't keep him from taking her in, although it meant ignoring his instinct to reassure her.

His eyes raked her frame, settling above the waist on the exposed expanse of creamy flesh. The air in the room dissipated, and he wanted to tug at the nowhere-near-tight neckline of the saffron leine his grandfather had given him to wear.

Eoin swallowed—twice. He was too hot.

Did the fire need to be banked?

He needed to look at the hearth to check, but he couldn't tear his eyes away from the petite blonde lass he'd kidnapped from the future.

She was… *Gorgeous* seemed too weak a term.

The gown he'd forbidden his sister from wearing was perfect on Ashlyn.

Made for Ashlyn.

Not only did it hug her slender torso and form to it, placing her breasts high and tempting, it flared at the hip, hinting at the rounded perfection there, and flowing down to the floor in a gracious way that made her even more attractive.

"Who is this vision?" Angus breathed, pushing to his feet with his hands held out.

"'Tis just me, Grandfa." Fiona beamed, true to her cheeky nature, and their grandfather chuckled.

The elderly man shook his head. "Yer bonnie, as ye well know, my lassie, but I dinnae refer ta ye, this time."

Ashlyn flushed that enchanting shade of crimson, and it lit the creamy skin of her neck and visible collarbones, too.

Made Eoin itch to run his fingers over every inch of her. He had to avert his gaze. His cock twitched. Which was ridiculous, considering he'd seen her clothed in *a whole lot* less than his sister's fancy dress.

The elderly charmer crossed the distance to Ashlyn and took both her hands in his. "Ye, lass, are a bonnie sight fer an old man."

"Th-th-thank you," she murmured, but she didn't look at his grandfather.

Her eyes found his and Eoin *needed* a distraction.

He couldn't very well ravish her in front of an audience, especially this one.

"What are *ye* doin' out a' yer chambers?" He tried to bark at his sister, but the question came out cracked.

Fiona's sweet smile was replaced by a glare so fast it should've made his head spin, but he was used to such flips from his little pest. "Grandfa dinnae agree with yer...orders."

He frowned.

"Now, now, no' in front a' tha guest," Angus said.

Eoin narrowed his eyes to his ever-the-peacemaker grandfather. "Ye dote on her —"

"Later, Eoin." The man's voice was hard.

Fiona harrumphed and her eyes were slits, daring him to defy the man who'd raised them.

Ashlyn froze, her unease obvious. She swayed in ladies' slippers that were no doubt Fiona's. She didn't pull away from their grandfather's grip, but Eoin's gut said she was just being polite.

"I *shall* have words wit' ye." He pointed at Fiona. "And ye." He pointed to their grandfather's chest. "As well as Jamie MacLeod." Maybe he'd replace his cousin as steward.

His sister's fists were balled at her sides. She wore a scowl that destroyed her beauty. "Ye are a barbar —"

"Lass, return ta yer quarters," Angus commanded. "We shall speak later, indeed." He looked at Eoin. "Jamie dinnae need be involved. Tha lad was followin' *my* orders."

Eoin frowned again. It wasn't fair to pit his cousin against his grandfather, who'd been the laird much longer than Eoin himself, but that only irritated him more. He grunted and swallowed some choice curses that would raise Angus' ire.

Fiona glowered before whirling away, her red skirts swooshing as she obeyed their grandfather, and fairly stomped to the door, which she slammed on her way out.

Ashlyn winced. "I'm sorry."

His grandfather's blue eyes were soft when he looked back at her. "Nay a need fer ye ta apologize, lass. 'Tis a family conflict. 'Twill be remedied shortly."

"She will *no'* marry a MacDonald," Eoin growled.

Angus sent him a silencing stare, then glanced back at Ashlyn. "Come, lass. Ne'er ye mind my lad here, or my granddaughter. Let us speak of yer journey."

"My...my...journey?" Ashlyn stuttered, but let the elderly man lead her toward the fire.

Eoin brought over a chair with a padded seat for her.

She looked at him as she sat but didn't thank him.

Not that he blamed her. He was still in the wrong, no matter how lovely she was in attire from his time.

He swallowed a sigh and carried the carved chair from his grandfather's desk closer to the warm fire. Eoin sat next to her, while Angus asked a few polite questions and Ashlyn answered quietly.

She looked overwhelmed, and with wide brown eyes and the slight tremor to her shoulders; no doubt she was just that.

Guilt swirled around his stomach, jumping up to form a lump in his throat. He didn't know what to say, so he kept his mouth shut. When he got her alone, she was probably going to flay him open as soon as she regained her composure. Since Eoin couldn't define a reason for his selfishness, he couldn't fathom what he'd say to her then, either.

"I'm Angus MacLeod, an' I used ta be laird, a 'fore this one. I'm grandfa to Eoin, an' the lovely lassie who left here in a huff."

Eoin snorted. Angus' obvious affection for him and his little bother was evident with the way the man spoke, despite what he'd said about his sister's current insolence.

"Nice…to meet you." Ashlyn gained strength with each passing second. She let his scoundrel of a grandfather kiss her knuckles, and her cheeks went pink all over again.

"We lost his da, my lad Gregor, when Eoin was a lad. So, I was laird again then, too. So, he could finish growin' an' learnin'." Even though it'd been nearly twenty years since his da had died, the elderly man's voice was lined with grief for his only child.

He missed his father, too. He'd been a great man. Firm, but loving, and he'd had magic. Eoin was often saddened Fiona had never gotten to meet either of their parents. She'd been raised right, but she'd still missed out. He'd at least had thirteen years with them.

"I'm so sorry." Ashlyn looked at Eoin, and the genuine sympathy she wore, shining in those dark eyes, made him sit taller.

His heart stuttered. He didn't deserve for her to look at him with anything but disdain. "'Twas a long time ago," he muttered.

"Where do ye hail from, lass?" his grandfather asked.

She averted her gaze back to the older man, then Ashlyn pinned her pretty brown eyes on him, her brow drawn tight. "Eoin?" she whispered.

He cleared his throat. "Ah, go on, lass. Ye can tell him tha truth."

"I'm from the future."

"I ken it. Whereabou's?" The elderly man's demeanor was gentle.

Maybe Ashlyn needed kid-gloves at the moment. She blinked. He couldn't have just—

Wasn't he *surprised*?

Eoin's grandfather's statement was the last thing she'd expected. "Uh..."

How to answer him? He might've heard of the US, considering the colonies, but he wouldn't know what Texas was if she drew him a map.

Angus was looking at her expectantly. His eyes weren't the least bit clouded with age.

Eoin nudged her shoulder with his and she jumped.

She should yell at him, but Ashlyn couldn't muster anything intelligent. She hadn't been a fan when he'd put his chair so close moments before—or more accurately, she'd disliked the awareness that'd shivered down her spine—but she couldn't shift away without running into his grandfather's rocker. She was trapped between the two men.

She should be furious with him.

Ashlyn was, right?

"Texas," she whispered to Angus finally.

The old man leaned forward in his rocking chair and slapped his kilted thigh. "Texas?" he exclaimed.

"Texas mus' be a popular place ta leave," Eoin mumbled.

Ashlyn looked at her kidnapper, then at his grandfather and back. "What?"

The men exchanged a look, then the laird took an audible breath. "Ye...ye dinnae be the first lass ta come here from tha future." Eoin looked at his grandfather again, and the elderly man gave a nod.

I didn't come here. You *brought me here.*

She couldn't say that; she didn't want to get snarky in front of Angus. For the sake of manners and all that. "Okay...and?" she pushed out instead.

"From Texas," the laird said.

"What?" She cocked her head to one side, as if she had a hearing problem and the gesture would help.

Wrong.

Ashlyn gripped the arms of the chair and leaned forward.

As if it was possible, her current…situation…had just gotten more surreal.

They both started talking at once, but Eoin deferred to Angus, and the older man launched into a story full of magic, multiple instances of time travel, and the Fae — *flippin' fairies*. There was also information about the Faery Stones, the portal they'd used to come here.

The Faery Stones were the stalagmites with the unusual crystals on top of them in that cave. They'd looked unnatural because they were. Fae-born, not from what the elderly man called, *the Human Realm*.

Evidently, Eoin used the Stones a lot in fulfilling his duties as Guardian of the Faery Flag.

Ashlyn's instinct was to say, '*No freaking way*,' but she *was* sitting next to a big hearth where peat moss burned brightly, in a castle in Scotland, next to two oversized men wearing kilts. Then, there was also the 1755 part of her new reality.

Her head started spinning when Angus mentioned his aunt and her sister, *and* his wife all had been from the future — all three from Texas. A few other MacLeods were either Fae, or were from centuries other than the seventeenth or eighteenth, as well.

Oh, then the part that his mother had been a Fae Princess.

Like, an actual fairy—or, faery, as it was in Scotland.

"So, you're...not human?"

"I'm a halfling, as they say. My da, Alex, was human and the laird of Clan MacLeod for many years. Fae blood runs strong in my lad, here, too." He gestured to Eoin, who only nodded.

Angus said he'd had a younger sister, but that that was another story.

Whatever the heck *that* meant.

What was she supposed to say?

Ashlyn took a breath. "Do you mean to tell me that not one, not two, but three or *more* women who married into your family were from the future? My century, for the most part, too?"

The old man nodded, and his smile widened.

He'd told her he was ninety-two years old, and while years were definitely present in the lines of his face, he didn't look his age. Maybe seventy-five. Angus wasn't ancient-looking, or decrepit like a person nearly a century old should look.

"Aye, my Lila, God rest her soul, came from tha twenty-first century," the former laird said. "She was a healer—a skilled surgeon—and doctored many people around here for many years. She ran a clinic until she passed." The same grief was present in his tone as when he'd talked about his son.

So much loss, and Ashlyn felt awful for him, but he still wore a soft smile as he regarded her. He was a strong man—not unlike his grandson.

The word clinic jumped out...it wasn't an eighteenth-century word, so even if she hadn't believed him, its usage was a persuader. "So, this is like...the MacLeod thing?"

Angus stared at her with Eoin's eyes. If that wasn't disconcerting enough, the poor man probably had no idea what she'd just asked.

He surprised her by nodding. "If ye mean, has it been common, aye, t'has."

What the hell? floated around in her head again. It was becoming too common a recurring phrase, but Ashlyn would try to mind her manners and not say it aloud in front of Eoin's grandfather.

Women swearing wasn't a common thing in...these days...and she didn't want him to think she was rude. Fiona's warning was there, too, and she didn't want to offend him, either. The older man had a kind face, and like the women who'd bathed her, as well as Eoin's little sister, had been welcoming.

His hair was white and on the unkempt side—in need of a good cut, but she'd bet it'd been sable like Eoin's when he was a younger man. She could see the MacLeod resemblance, too.

Her hands opened and closed on the arms of the chair of their own accord as her mind went in circles, trying to make sense of all the information Angus had thrown at her. Would make a damn good book—or three. Ashlyn cleared her throat, but nothing surfaced to speak aloud.

Eoin shifting his big body on the chair next to hers caught her eye, and she spared him a glance. Even uncomfortable, he was breathtaking.

He'd put on a shirt—and wasn't that a shame?

She should be angry at him for all of this, but she couldn't muster anything past attraction and fascination. Apprehension had subsided, partly because she didn't fear for her safety. Like in the bath earlier, she was confident no one would hurt her here.

Ashlyn should roll her eyes at herself—feeling secure with her *kidnapper* and his family was crazy, but she did.

Hopefully that's not misplaced positive thinking.

"Are ye well, lass? I ken this is much ta take in," Angus said, again with that quiet and even tone that just washed more calm over her body.

She nodded. "I think so."

Eoin made a noise in his throat but didn't speak.

"Tell me abou' ye, lass," the elderly man said. His smile was open and encouraging, and somehow made her *want* to give the information he sought.

"I'm a writer. I…write books."

How would he take that, in an age when most women couldn't read, let alone write?

"Go on," Angus said, his expression sincere, like

he was genuinely interested. He actually wanted to know more. Also, it was as if he'd completely understood what she'd meant.

Ashlyn confessed her love of history, and Scotland particularly, and gave him the elevator pitch of her two completed trilogies that took place in the Highlands.

She explained she was currently working on the third book of her third trilogy, also about Scotland, but one hundred years after the first two sets of books.

His delight was evident in his posture as she talked about her stories, the ones inspired by Clan MacLeod specifically. He inclined his body forward, soaking up her every word. "Yer lass is a *seanchaí*, Eoin-lad!" He slapped his thigh again and rocked forward in his chair.

Her body flushed with heat, the corset constricted her breathing, and she tried not to wince when her heart skipped.

The protest was born in her head, *I'm not his lass,* but she didn't verbalize.

Ashlyn could feel Eoin's uneasiness as he fidgeted on his chair again, but the laird didn't open his mouth, either.

She avoided looking at him and met Angus's gaze. "Well, not really…I mean, kinda, I guess. I'm a storyteller, but I tell love stories. Romance; happily ever afters. I think that Gaelic term…means more."

Both men froze.

"Ye speak Gaelic?" Eoin asked.

Ashlyn shook her head. "No, but I understand some things. Endearments, and some…" Her cheeks heated and she rubbed the back of her neck. She'd had to do research for books. Didn't exactly want to admit that.

The laird's gaze locked with hers, and his Adam's apple bobbed as if he'd swallowed. "Some, what?" he whispered.

No way was she revealing she knew how to say, *I love you*, in Gaelic. The words floated into her head unbidden. *Tha gaol agam ort.* She'd watched a YouTube video about a hundred times in order to understand the pronunciation. Learning Gaelic had always been on her bucket list, too.

What would he say to *that*, anyway? It wasn't like it mattered. Shouldn't bother her, either.

Ashlyn cleared her throat again and looked back at Angus. "That's why I was in Scotland in the first place. A writer inspiration trip."

They probably wouldn't understand the concept of vacation, so she didn't go there.

"'Tis a lovely paintin' of my lad, ye found." He reached for the canvas from a small table beside him. Unrolled it and studied the image of his grandson. "Glad ta see it survived tha years."

"Ah, thanks. I like it very much." She could feel Eoin's stare but didn't want to look at him. She'd probably light up, blushing to her ears — something that was way too common around the stupid man.

The Faery Flag sat folded on the corner of the tiny table, and she stared for a moment, wanting to explore it, but didn't have the guts to ask.

It meant so much to Clan MacLeod. A sacred relic. Ashlyn had been fascinated with the legend behind it for years when she'd discovered the stories. She could ask Angus about it, if she ever got the courage to do so. Instinct told her he'd love to gush about it.

She wished she had paper and a pen. The man could be a walking, talking encyclopedia, if she'd let him.

"Where did ye come across tha paintin' a' my lad an' our Flag, anaway?"

"At an antique shop in Inverness."

Eoin jolted. "Enchanted Keepsakes, by chance?" His voice was just short of a demand.

She whipped around to meet his beckoning gaze, and her tummy fluttered at the intensity in her expression.

You really have to stop jumping when you just look at him. Focus on the whole kidnapping thing, dummy!

"How did you know?" Ashlyn croaked.

"Was there a lass called Korinna?"

"I don't know her name, but there was only one person in the shop."

"Bonnie lass, wit' flame-colored locks?" Eoin asked.

Ashlyn forced a nod, but she didn't like him

calling another woman pretty. Again, something that shouldn't trouble her, but did. She tried not to frown.

He said something in Gaelic under his breath, and his grandfather frowned, but his mouth rippled, as if he was holding back amusement.

"Lad, dinnae say such things around a lady, even if she dinnae understand 'em. Besides, ye already suspected 'twas the witch, dinnae?"

Eoin didn't look like he appreciated the admonition, but he gave a curt nod.

"Witch?" Ashlyn asked.

"Ye tell her, I'm too angry." He gestured for good measure.

"Dinnae fash yerself, lad. What's done is done." Angus nodded.

"I don't know if I can handle magic, time travel, the Fae, *and* witches all being real," she said.

The elderly man threw his head back and laughed. "Poor lass. 'Tis all real; witches, too. I ne'er met her, but from wha' I hear, Korinna is a powerful witch."

Eoin nodded and sighed. He ran his hand through his hair, mussing his dark locks and making her want to slip her fingers there instead.

Cursing herself didn't dispel the urge. Ashlyn must be a fickle weakling if she could let her attraction to him override good sense.

Kidnapping *was* illegal, wasn't it?

At least in *her* time. She *shouldn't* forgive him,

right?

"Aye, she is," the laird said. "She vowed I would ne'er have ta run tha centuries chasin' tha Faery Flag." Eoin launched into a story from three years before.

They'd met on one of his missions to retrieve the Flag. His frustration was evident when his broad shoulders tightened. He made a fist and pinned it to his lap as he spoke.

She couldn't tear her eyes away. Ashlyn almost forgot Angus was in the room.

Eoin's brogue was thick, but his voice was smooth, and she caught herself leaning toward him sometime during the recital.

She needed to get closer, but caught herself, sitting taller and pressing into the back of her chair.

A part of her didn't like the way he'd talked about the ethereal beauty she'd met in the shop. Especially when he explained how he'd learned all about technology and modern conveniences from the woman. All that stuff implied they'd spent a great deal of time together.

Had they been lovers?

Ashlyn frowned.

Stop. It wouldn't matter if they had.

Eoin had kissed her twice.

Her stomach flipped and she tried to banish the memories of his taste, the heat of his body and how his chest—and the rest of him—looked. How hard his muscles had felt against her. Especially that one part of him that'd been…well, hard.

Be mad at him, Ashlyn Elaine George. Stay *mad at him!*

"Tha witch put tha Flag wit' yer paintin' a' purpose," Angus said, tugging her from Forbidden Land.

Ashlyn should thank him; thoughts of naked Eoin were useless. It wasn't like she was going to sleep with him. It took her mind a second to catch up and process what the older man had said.

"Aye, I'd gathered," Eoin said.

"But why?" she blurted.

The laird and his grandfather exchanged a look she didn't understand.

Angus sat taller and stilled his gentle movements of the rocking chair. He pinned them both with his very blue gaze.

A quiver went down Ashlyn's spine before his lips even parted.

"Fate," he whispered.

What the hell does that mean?

chapter eleven

oin puzzled over what his Grandfa had said about fate for hours. He hadn't said much at the evening meal down in the great hall.

The word reverberated in his head, in English and Gaelic.

Was Ashlyn his…fate?

He was well educated in the family legends regarding the women who'd married into his clan from other centuries but had never considered them more than stories from the past. As much as he time traveled, he'd never contemplated a lass for himself being from the future. Hell, he hardly ever contemplated a lass for himself at all. Not for keeps, anyway.

Eoin had needs of course, but he always found a woman to assuage them. He was a considerate lover, making sure she had pleasure, too, but he never stayed beyond his purpose, and had *never* been tempted for more.

Marriage was always in the back of his mind, of course. He needed an heir, and would have to wed eventually, but Angus only mentioned it every so often, not really pressuring him.

He was only thirty. He had time.

Ashlyn was seated next to him as an honored guest, and his lass hadn't said much since they'd climbed up the dais to take their places, either. Perhaps she was contemplating what Angus had said as well, or mayhap she was still taking everything in.

She'd pushed the venison around on her plate, too, but Nessie had fussed her into eating a portion of it after a while.

Fiona laughed loudly at something someone said, and he shot his sister a look, but she flashed a grin, unrepentant as usual, with her dimple showing.

She hadn't cornered him regarding the MacDonald lad, so the fact she was of a pleasant disposition could mean she was scheming, or she felt their grandfather would help fulfill her wishes.

It wouldn't work. Eoin wouldn't change his mind.

He could feel someone watching him and swung his eyes around until they collided with Angus', as if the man had guessed he'd been thinking of him. Maybe he had. His grandfather had the uncanny ability to sense emotions, but he wasn't quite the empath his mother was said to have been.

At least he couldn't read minds, like some of their cousins with Fae blood. That would've been disastrous.

He offered a nod and Eoin returned it, but the elderly man's gaze didn't waver. He was watching the lass next to Eoin, too.

Fate?

Eoin shook the thought away. It was likely to drive him mad if he didn't let it go.

Fiona was chatting with her—but at least Ashlyn was talking, then smiling. Even the occasional laugh.

His little pest had seemed to have charmed his honey-haired lass like she did everyone else. Maybe she had magic after all, and it lay with her interactions with others.

He didn't like the feeling of jealousy that lingered. His sister had made her laugh, instead of him. Eoin tried to subtly watch her, but that melted into a full-out stare. Ashlyn was enchanting as she gestured and shared words with Fiona as well as their grandfather.

So beautiful he couldn't breathe. She was still clad in the green gown, and sitting pushed her breasts higher, their perfection giving him more nourishment than the food he'd consumed.

"Eoin?"

He jumped when Angus called his name. From the concern on his grandfather's face, it hadn't been the first time.

"What?" He winced. He'd not meant to bark.

"Nessie's been tryin' ta hand ye a plate, ye big oaf," Fiona snapped.

Heat kissed the back of his neck. His cheeks burned and he wanted to curse. He was probably red.

When was the last time he'd *blushed*?

Eoin threw what he hoped was an apologetic look

to the housekeeper. Wanted to rub his embarrassment away but didn't.

"Yer favorite, my laird." The older woman lifted a trencher full of cakes, tarts, and sweet breads to him.

He muttered thanks and returned her smile. Maybe it would help him feel less like he'd gone daft.

"Try these." His sister was bright again, as she reached and put two pieces of sweet bread on Ashlyn's plate. "Apple is Eoin's favorite, I fancy tha spiced."

His lass turned a wide smile to Fiona that again made him feel a stab in his gut. When would she give *him* a smile like that?

Eoin couldn't tear his gaze away as Ashlyn brought the slice of bread to her lips and took a bite, then her little pink tongue darted out to catch a morsel at the corner of her mouth.

She closed her eyes as she took another bite. Her little moan of appreciation was his undoing.

He ordered his manhood to stand down. Then again, *stand* was the wrong choice of words. He cleared his throat and averted his gaze. Forced his fingers to close around the apple tart, then shoved it into his mouth and chewed. He couldn't seem to appreciate the flavor bursting on his taste buds like he usually did.

"Oh my. This is awesome!"

"She likes it!" Fiona grinned, and Nessie beamed.

"Thanks, Nessie," Ashlyn said.

"I dinnae do all tha cookin', but no one can match my sweets," the housekeeper said.

"I believe it!" his lass exclaimed.

The meal couldn't end soon enough.

Eoin couldn't sit still, and his family — especially his grandfather — kept throwing him knowing looks. The glances from Fiona were annoyed, but he couldn't very well tell his sister all the blood in his body had settled below his waist.

When the lasses started removing the trenchers, he shot to his feet.

Angus arched a furry white eyebrow, and even Ashlyn sent him a questioning look.

"C'mon, lass. I'll walk ye ta yer quarters," Eoin told her.

"Oh. Okay." She looked at his sister and grandfather. "Thank you for the lovely company and the good meal."

"G'night, lass."

His sister smiled as if she'd made a fast friend, and with his little pest, that was probably true. She echoed Angus' evening wishes, and finally Eoin was alone with Ashlyn.

He resisted the urge to rest his hand at the small of her back. Touching her was a bad idea, especially since he couldn't get the taste of her mouth out of his memory. Watching her eat Nessie's famous desserts had been a mistake.

Eoin had meant to take her to the rooms next to his. The rooms that would be his wife's when he finally wed and had a connecting interior door to his own.

However, the entry he stopped outside of was the laird's chambers. He pushed the door open and gestured for Ashlyn to enter in front of him.

Her brow was knitted. "But…this is the room I was in earlier. The room I bathed and dressed in."

"Aye," he croaked.

"I thought…I thought…these were your rooms."

"Aye."

Her cheeks reddened. "I can't stay with you, Eoin."

Instinct was for him to shout, '*Why not?*' or worse, order her to do just that, but he couldn't. She'd be angrier with him than she already had the right to be. "There're rooms adjoinin' ta my own." He pointed to the nearby door. "Ye'll stay there."

"Oh. Then why—?" Ashlyn indicated her surroundings. His things.

Eoin couldn't confess he just wasn't ready to part from her company. An unmanly shiver traversed his limbs, and he cleared his throat. He'd lost track of how many times he'd done *that* all evening. "I needed ta speak with ye a'fore we retire, s'all."

She cocked her head to one side, studying him. "About what? We've been talking all day."

Ashlyn was right, and it was nothing that couldn't wait until the morn.

It didn't matter; he couldn't let her go, even if she'd be close by, sleeping in a bed that was not his own.

Eoin frowned.

"What's wrong?" she whispered.

"Nothin'." It was too quick if her expression was any indication. "I'm tryin' ta apologize ta ye," he blurted. That was only half true.

He shifted in his deerskin boots at the end of his bed, and his calf bumped into the trunk that housed his clothing. Eoin avoided looking at his oversized four-poster bed. If he gave the MacLeod tartan and lush furs too much notice, Ashlyn would think he wanted her in his bed.

Which he did, but surely, she wouldn't be agreeable.

"What for?" Her pretty face was open, honest.

Wasn't she angry at him for kidnapping her?

"I brought ye here, lass. Against yer will." Eoin held his breath, awaiting her answer.

"I'm not mad." Ashlyn caressed the smooth carved wood of the closest bedpost and tried not to look at him. "I mean, I probably should be. Scratch that, I *know* I should be...but this is a gift, really."

She was probably crazy after all, but sometime over the evening any anger she had for Eoin had melted into enchantment for where—*when*—she was. She couldn't put her finger on the why, but didn't want to examine it, either.

"A...gift?"

Ashlyn nodded. "I've been writing about seventeenth and eighteenth-century Scotland for years. I could've never fathomed that I'd *see* it with my own eyes. For real. Magic…is real."

"Aye, 'tis."

She laughed and shook her head. "Time travel. And the Fae. Wow."

"Are…are ye sure yer…well?"

When she finally met his gaze, the laird looked confused. She'd never seen Eoin MacLeod unsure. She didn't like the look on him or her instant urge to make *him* feel better. He was shifting in his boots like a little kid in trouble.

Yup, I've lost my mind.

Ashlyn closed her eyes and released a breath that pushed against the corset of Fiona's gown. She sensed Eoin's presence, felt the heat coming off his body.

He'd come closer to her.

She opened her eyes and found his.

He was standing only inches away, and she wanted to reach for him. When she should still want to smack him and shove him from her, all she could do was look at his mouth and remember what it was like to kiss him.

Dammit.

"I *should* want to go home now; you kidnapped me."

Eoin winced when she said the *K-word*. "Lass, I—"

"It's okay, Eoin. I…want to stay, at least for a little while. Could I get some paper—parchment—and something to write with?"

If he was surprised by the request, he hid it well. "Aye, lass. Anathin'."

"Do you think Angus would…tell me stories? Answer questions? I could write some things down…"

"Aye, I ken he would."

"I was kinda hoping he'd enjoy it, really," Ashlyn whispered.

"Aye, I believe he would."

Her heart skipped at the intensity in Eoin's eyes. "Are you angry that I want to…document the real Clan MacLeod? I've done a lot of research. Written about your clan and the Isle of Skye, even the MacLeods of Lewis. I just…talking to Angus would be the *real* thing. I could see what's true and what's not. Plus, he can tell me about the Fae. And…magic."

He shook his head. "Nay, lass."

"Then…is something wrong?"

"Why do ye ask?"

"You're looking at me…funny." Awareness skittered over all her nerve endings and made her heart stutter. Ashlyn swallowed. Tried to make herself stand still.

"Ye…lass."

"Eoin?"

"*Ye* are tha gift, lass."

Heat suffused her face and neck for the millionth

time. Ashlyn went to shake her head, but Eoin reached out, dragging two fingers down her cheek and it took all she was made of not to erase the small distance between them and burrow into his chest.

He must've bathed before dinner, because his hair was damp, and he smelled so good. Fresh sandalwood and sage washed over her senses.

She stood there like an idiot, next to the big bed she should probably move away from, before she did something stupid, like grab his hand and drag him to it. Beg Eoin to kiss her again, touch her all over, and make love to her.

You don't even know him, idiot.

Angus said fate had brought her to 1755, and the idea had haunted Ashlyn's brain since that afternoon.

What was fate?

Meeting Eoin?

Wanting him with a hunger she'd never felt for another man?

She wasn't a one-night-stand kinda girl. She'd had lovers, all of whom she'd been in *relationships* with.

If Ashlyn went there with the laird, it'd be no better than a few nights. She was going home to the future; she'd leave him behind. It wasn't like they could have a *real* relationship. Could she kiss him and see where it went?

Who are you trying to kid? You know where it'd go.

Them. Naked. Entangled. With a likely repeat.

He'd be as good as one of her romance novel

heroes.

Ashlyn trembled.

They *couldn't* be together long term. It was impossible, but the idea that they were doomed before they could start *hurt* somehow. Which didn't make sense.

How can I feel so much for him?

Nothing made sense, even though she'd processed the time travel part. The 1755 part, the magic part. Ashlyn was still working on understanding all Angus had said about the Fae.

She'd bought a picture of Eoin, then met him that very night.

If that wasn't fate, what was?

Just magic?

Ashlyn fidgeted in Fiona's slippers.

Stop staring at him and say something before he thinks you're the idiot you are.

"I don't know why I want to say this, but I do," she whispered.

"What, lass?"

"Thank you, Eoin. For bringing me here."

He shook his head, making his sable locks dance over his shoulders. "Nay, lass. I dinnae deserve tha'." His expression was serious, with a touch of sadness, but there was more there, too. Something that darkened his eyes.

Ashlyn burned to run her fingers through his hair, and caress his face, touch his neck and chest, then more. Desire settled low and hot, making her legs shake and her core throb, and she tried to shake free, but couldn't look away from the intensity in his sapphire gaze.

chapter twelve

"**b**ut you do," she whispered. "It's…not how I planned my trip to Scotland, but…the surprise is awesome, I guess. Fulfills the purpose of my visit, really. In more ways than you could know."

Eoin swallowed and fell into her fathomless brown eyes. His Ashlyn was so sincere, so forgiving when he was *so* wrong. He would grant her *anything* in his power. He wanted to. More than that, he *needed* to.

She'd forgiven him.

Ashlyn really was a gift.

"I make ye a vow, lass." Eoin's heart sped up, and it took all he was made of to stand there and say what he was thinking. Words he didn't want to be true, but they had to be.

For his Ashlyn. Because he couldn't be an honorless bastard. Any longer than he'd already been.

"A vow?"

Wisps of her blonde hair had escaped the fancy style one of the lasses had done for her, and his fingers itched to caress them, tuck them behind her ear, or yank the pins out so he could see the golden waves free, dancing about. Run his hands through the thick locks and bring her closer.

Taste her mouth. Take *her*.

"Aye." Eoin forced a nod. "When yer done with whate'er ye need here, I'll take ye back. Ta yer own time."

Even though it'll kill me to see you walk away.

The strength of his feelings made no sense. He'd seen this lass at the pub in twenty-first century Inverness, then brought her back home on what? A whim?

He inhaled, but it didn't make his head stop spinning. His grandfather's voice popped into his thoughts with that dreaded word.

Fate.

Ashlyn arched an eyebrow and studied him. She pursed her lips, then sucked in an audible breath. "Okay."

Eoin couldn't stop watching her mouth, and he needed to. Being here in his rooms, by his bed, was worse than watching her eat sweet bread. Too much to resist. He wanted to rip his sister's gown off her.

Ashlyn stepped closer and his cock twitched.

Closer was bad, too tempting, but he wouldn't have moved away if an enemy had had a sword in his back.

"So, you're promising that this is all on my terms?"

Eoin nodded, his eyes sliding to how her breasts moved up and down in the corset when she breathed.

"Okay," Ashlyn repeated.

Her voice drew his gaze back to her face. Her cheeks were flushed with color again.

His thoughts scattered because her breasts heaved once more. *Damn,* he needed to kiss her.

"Can you…show me to my room?"

Eoin jumped—then cursed himself to hell and back. "Aye."

She smiled.

His heart skipped and he had to swallow.

Do not touch her.

If he did, he wouldn't be showing her anywhere but to his own bed, and Eoin couldn't. That certainly wouldn't be something on *her* terms.

He'd made more than one vow to his Ashlyn this night.

She walked ahead of him after he led her through the door. A helpful servant—probably Nessie—had lit the fire in the hearth, so the room was warm and had a welcoming glow. It was smaller than his, but he'd always liked this chamber.

The furniture was dark wood, matching his own, but it had feminine touches in the carvings, and it wasn't so oversized, like what was in the laird's suite.

He remembered afternoons here, spending time snuggled in his mother's arms when he was a wee laddie. She'd had a wonderful laugh, his mother. Fiona's smile looked just like Lady Eleanor's. 'Twas a shame his sister had never gotten to know the woman who'd birthed them. She'd been quiet and loving, and he missed her.

Eoin had never—and would never—admitted it to a soul, but the day he'd left to foster with the Clan MacKinnon, he'd bawled like a bairn when his mother had released him from a long hug. He'd been a laddie, but too old to shed tears over missing his mother.

"This quilt is beautiful!" Ashlyn caressed the fluffy bedding, which consisted of a MacLeod tartan stuffed and embroidered with heathers and thistles.

"My mother made it."

Silence fell as she whirled and stood by the bed, wringing her hands in front of her. Then she jerked them behind her. "Umm, I think I can take it from here. Good night, Eoin. Sleep well."

He forced his head to nod. "If ye need anathin', ye dinnae have ta knock. Come ta me."

"I will."

Eoin practically fled the room, almost tripping over his feet. He needed to retreat and stop imagining Ashlyn undressing or donning the sleeping gown folded on the trunk at the end of the bed that had been his mother's.

Thoughts of Lady Eleanor should cool his ardor regarding the honey-haired lass, but it didn't. He remembered every inch of Ashlyn's bare skin against his when he'd held her in the cave of the Faery Stones. The taste of her kiss preoccupied him, and he wanted to experience it again. Then so much more.

He shut the adjoining door with a resounding *thud.*

Eoin's fingers made quick work of his belt, and he slid the plaid from around his waist. Normally he slept in the nude, but he didn't dare with Ashlyn so close, so he pulled soft short pants from his trunk and slipped them on. He tossed the yellow leine, then remembered it was Angus', and folded it. Set it on his trunk with a mental note to have Nessie or Peg return it to his grandfather after laundering.

He didn't expect to sleep. He was half-aroused, his cock making itself known with his every movement. The organ wasn't concerned with sorting through the chaos in his head about Ashlyn. It just wanted her. To be inside her. He turned down his bedding with a sigh.

The knock on the connecting door made him freeze.

"Eoin?" Ashlyn's soft call penetrated the wood panel.

"Come," he called. Eoin's heart and his manhood jolted with the door's creak when she pushed her way into his room.

Her eyes raked his frame and she stilled, stopping right inside. "Oh. You're already ready for bed. I'm sorry—"

He stepped away from his bed. "What's wrong, Ashlyn?" He liked the way her name rolled off his tongue. He should say it more often.

She shuddered and rubbed her arm.

"Lass?" Eoin whispered.

"I, um…I…can't get out of this dress. Alone."

Oh. Shite.

He was about to come out of his own skin. Eoin should call some of the lasses. He shouldn't—

"C'mere, lass, an' I shall help ye." The words were his own, but they were so *wrong*.

"I'm sorry for asking, the ties are on the back, I tried…" Ashlyn shrugged, and it lifted her tempting breasts yet again.

"'Tis fine." He gestured and she obeyed, giving him her back so he could open the fine bodice.

Eoin subtly sucked in air, bidding his head to stop spinning. Her shoulders were already bare, and he longed to lean down and taste her skin. His fingers shook when he reached for the green ribbon. He fumbled but got the job done as best he could.

She lifted her hands, holding the loosening fabric to the front of her body, and he wanted to beg her to let it drop to the floor.

"Thanks," Ashlyn whispered. She turned and spared Eoin a glance that resulted in their gazes locking.

She swallowed and the need to kiss her throat burned.

"Anathin' fer ye, lass." Even to his own ears, his voice was gruff, full of desire.

Ashlyn flushed and fidgeted, pinning the green

fabric over her perfect breasts. "Good night, my laird." His lass retreated to the lady's chamber, but her parting phrase had him hard and aching.

He couldn't move. Eoin stared at the door she'd left ajar.

Go to bed, you wretch.

Before he could assure himself of the useless sod he was, the adjoining panel swung open again.

Ashlyn stood before him, her hair down and loose, wearing nothing but the ivory sleeping gown. The light behind her from the hearth gave her a golden aura that sucked away his breath. The fabric wasn't diaphanous, but he could see her barely covered curves.

His heart thundered and his blood rushed south. If he'd wanted her before, the yearning was now tenfold. His cock ached, and he wasn't wearing a leine or plaid to hide it. Eoin didn't dare glance down. His short pants were no doubt tented.

"Ashlyn?" Her name fell from his mouth.

"Eoin…I…" She worried her bottom lip. "I…don't want to be alone. Can I sleep with you?"

God's Blood, I'm doomed.

Ashlyn called herself every weak name she could think of. Was she really standing there, begging a guy she'd met less than twenty-four hours ago to *sleep* with him?

As in share his bed, not his body. Although she couldn't deny she wanted him.

Eoin wasn't wearing anything except a pair of ivory shorts that stopped at his knees. They clung to his powerful thighs. The closest thing to eighteenth century boxers there were.

Her eyes trailed his body, making note of what she'd seen before; huge pecs dotted with black curls, a happy trail dividing an eight-pack and disappearing into the fabric at his waist. Springy coarse hair continuing down his legs.

Not to mention…he was aroused.

She tried not to gulp.

Turn around. Go back to the other room. Tell him never mind.

Ashlyn *couldn't* have sex with him.

What would he say if she told him no? He was obviously ready.

"Aye." His voice was thicker than normal, but when Eoin gestured to the bed, it was as if his hand commanded her bare feet.

She went to him in silence, feeling naked despite the chemise that fell to her ankles and had long sleeves. A higher neckline than the one she'd worn beneath Fiona's gown. Ashlyn had nothing on *under* it.

Watching his Adam's apple bob told her Eoin was struggling. Holding himself back.

Is that good or bad?

Tingles darted all over her body. She wasn't the

least bit afraid of him. He'd never hurt her; she'd felt that from the start.

However, if he stole a kiss, she'd be a goner. Unable to tell him no. She'd give herself to him in a heartbeat, and that made Ashlyn feel...out of control.

Why doesn't it feel wrong? I don't know him.

"Thank you." The whisper fell from her lips, and she moved past him to climb onto the fat feather mattress. She heard a groan behind her, and the back of her neck went hot enough to combust. She'd just pulled a crawling-on-all-fours with Eoin obviously watching. Inadvertently given him a show. Hopefully all that fabric covered her ass.

He didn't say anything, but there was a lot of grunting before he joined her in the bed, and he placed his body as far from her as physically possible. On the far edge.

Ashlyn was making him uncomfortable in his own bed, but she didn't want to leave.

Awkwardness settled over them, and she spared him a glance. Tried to smile. "What happens while I'm here?"

Eoin cleared his throat and turned to his side, facing her. He bent his arm and propped his head up with his palm, and she couldn't help but watch the play of his defined muscles as he moved. "What d'ye mean?"

"To my time. I'm...worried about Kate. She's going to freak when I'm not there...what happened? I don't remember." She frowned.

"I put ye both ta sleep with magic. Dinnae fash, I placed her in tha cottage in bed. She's safe."

"You followed us!" Ashlyn poked his chest.

His expression was half-amused, half-embarrassed. "Aye," he confessed. "My magic confirmed ye had tha Flag."

"You knew it was in my painting?"

Eoin smirked. "My paintin'."

Ashlyn stuck her tongue out but froze when his eyes slid to her lips and stayed. She swallowed, but it didn't help; her mouth had gone dry. She had to pant to breathe.

"I…" He leaned forward as he trailed off, giving her the chance to retreat.

She didn't.

Ashlyn closed the distance between them and pressed her mouth to his.

He took it from there, drawing her into his chest and pushing his tongue deep, touching hers tentatively.

This kiss wasn't like the other two; it was softer, gentler, perhaps a question.

She wrapped her tongue around his and slid her arms around his neck. Ashlyn answered his query with a resounding '*yes*'. Moved closer, kissing him harder.

Eoin's hands made their way down her back, aligning their bodies until he was kneading her bottom and pressing his erection into her stomach. He tugged the chemise up, up, up. In seconds his hands would be on her bare skin. His fingertips brushed the back of her thighs, and Ashlyn shivered.

She moaned, but the cautious part of her brain piped up and told her to move away before things got farther than she could handle. She broke their kiss on a whimper and stared into his eyes. Put her hands on his bare chest and felt the thundering of his heart. "I'm sorry. We just met. I-I-I...can't."

Not yet anyway.

Ashlyn couldn't tell him that.

If Eoin was disappointed, he hid it well. "Lass—"

"Maybe I should just go to the other room."

"Nay. Nay." His pecs heaved against her as he inhaled. "I wish ye ta stay. I'd ne'er force ye."

"I know," Ashlyn whispered. "I know you wouldn't hurt me."

"Ne'er."

Silence descended and she hollered at herself to move out of the circle of his arms. She couldn't make herself go. She quivered.

"Are ye cold?"

Ashlyn shook her head. "Not with you holding me."

"Good."

She needed a distraction, and he'd never answered her. "So, what happens to my time while I'm here?"

"I will return ye ta tha moment I took ye, an' nothin' will be fer tha worse."

"Ah. Will I remember?"

"Aye, unless you wish otherwise."

"What d'you mean?"

Eoin's gaze roved her face and made her heart skip. "I could make ye ferget. With magic, if ye wished it."

I would never want to forget you.

Besides, that'd make her much anticipated research irrelevant. "Oh." Ashlyn bit her bottom lip. She heard a soft groan and stilled against him.

Eoin flashed a small smile. It looked strained.

"Are you sure you don't want me to go?"

"I want ye wit' me."

She swallowed again. Ashlyn *wanted* to be with him. In more ways than she had courage for. "Okay."

"Close yer eyes, Ash, go ta sleep."

His use of her nickname made her pause, but she couldn't help her smile. A small pang made her miss Kate. "You're sure everything will be okay…there…with me here?"

"Aye, lass." His words were low, and when she glanced up at him, he'd shut his eyes.

Eoin rolled to his back, but kept her pinned to his side, with his arm around her.

Ashlyn stared at his handsome face until his breathing fell into a deep and even rhythm.

Her belly fluttered. Warmth, from his body where

it touched hers, as well as the feeling of safety. Nothing could happen to her if she stayed in his arms.

Is this my fate?

She was afraid of the answer, so she left the question dangling in her head.

chapter thirteen

shlyn spent the next morning obsessing about Eoin. She'd watched him spar with his men in the bailey, his sister at her side until the teen had gotten bored and went off with the MacLeod servants.

The laird was a beast with a sword in his hand, but graceful, too, in a way she never would've attached to hand-to hand combat.

When the men had worked up enough sweat to shed their shirts despite the chilly morning, she couldn't tear her eyes away from Eoin. The play of his muscles as he moved like a dancer, thrusting his huge weapon, rushing forward and back. He parried and clashed the sword against the men's over and over, sometimes even taking on more than one at a time.

Eoin was better than any romance hero she'd ever come up with.

So hot. That she'd already known, Ashlyn had eyes—and hands—after all, but to see him interact with his men, some of them no doubt family, warmed her from the inside out. He laughed with them, showed open affection with arms over shoulders and shared playful punches and shoves, like friends in a locker room.

He was a fierce fighter, a good leader, a good laird, and the other guys obviously adored him.

A good man.

My fate?

How?

It was hard to breathe. She couldn't help but remember last night, sleeping in his bed. In his arms.

Ashlyn was a fool for rejecting him, yet she was equally foolish to consider sex with a stranger from the eighteenth century. Especially since there weren't condoms, or her birth control pills handy.

Eoin doesn't feel like a stranger.

"Lass, I've been lookin' fer ye everawhere!" Angus' yell made her jump — and look away from her object of desire.

"Coming!" She made her way to the elderly man, away from the small area of tiers set up along the fence in the bailey.

Eoin's grandfather regaled her with tales of winged men, Fae Warriors, and incredible magic as soon as they'd gotten to his rooms. Angus even spoke of pink and purple trees, blue and orange grass in the Fae Realm.

He'd been delighted when she'd asked if he'd be willing to help her research for future books. Although he hadn't looked all that surprised. The laird had probably talked to him about it.

Eoin had come through with his promise and had

presented Angus with supplies for Ashlyn; a stack of parchment and as much ink as she wanted. Even three different quills to write with.

She'd been able to take notes when she talked to the elderly man.

Listening to Angus speak was as enthralling as his subject matter, like a spell. Not only because of his brogue, but that was part of her fascination. However, the man was a hell of a storyteller, and she hung on his every word. A walking, talking history book, and he loved to share anything Clan MacLeod, and his knowledge in general, as well as all the magic stuff.

He spoke fondly of his parents, regaling her with the story of how they'd met. It would make a hell of a good book—full of forbidden love, danger, and evil plots, and finally happily ever after.

However, Ashlyn missed Eoin.

Was he avoiding her?

He'd been gone from his bed before she'd woken, and disappointment had washed over her. She wanted to see him, speak with him.

Kiss him again.

Oh. Stop. You rejected him last night.

Afternoon rolled into evening, and Ashlyn had at least gotten to see him at supper. She'd been seated next to him up on the dais, and he was attentive. Somewhat talkative, but it left her needing more. Eoin had been too polite and proper, seeming to ensure he didn't touch her.

When they'd retired, she'd climbed into his bed without much conversation.

He hadn't reached for her and hurt settled low in her belly. He'd bid her a whispered goodnight, then presented her with his back.

Ashlyn had tried not to cry, and sleep was fleeting that night. Despite his presence beside her, she'd felt alone for the first time since he'd brought her to 1755. Calling herself names didn't fix her mixed feelings, either.

She'd rejected him after all, so it made sense that he would pull away. That didn't make her feel better. Not to mention the level of how hurt she felt was ridiculous.

The next three days passed with the same routine, leaving her aching for more of the laird than the few words exchanged over meals and sleeping next to him in the big bed.

She'd woken in his arms the night before and watched the rise and fall of his bare muscled chest. She hadn't had the guts to kiss him but had burned to do so.

Eoin must've reached for her in his sleep.

Ashlyn rolled over and opened her eyes, groaning and cursing the stupid thoughts running on a pathetic loop in her head. Like a bad dream.

Night *four* in the past. She couldn't sleep.

Warmth bled into her side through her nightgown. It was good, because it was Eoin, but he still hadn't touched her on purpose. Being against his body again was almost as good as the first night at Dunvegan, but he'd obviously retreated for a reason.

She propped herself up over his chest and gnawed her bottom lip. Ashlyn stared. *Hurting.* Even though that was stupid. "How can I miss you when you're right here?"

Eoin stirred and blinked. "Lass?" The whisper was thick with sleep.

She cursed herself and embarrassment kissed her cheeks. Couldn't feign sleep, either, since she was hanging over him like some sort of stalker.

Dammit.

Ashlyn hadn't meant to wake him.

He yawned and pushed himself to a sitting position, taking her with him. Eoin slipped his arm around her shoulders. It was the first time he'd initiated physical contact since that first night.

Her heart missed a beat. "Why have you pushed me away?" she blurted, then winced.

"What, lass?"

"You…you've been avoiding me. I spend the days with Angus, missing you, despite all the interesting things he tells me. I…want to spend time with you, too."

Eoin didn't answer, but his gaze raked her face, as if he was trying to process her accusation/confession.

Mortification made words rush out. "I'm sorry, I shouldn't have—"

"Ashlyn." He cupped her cheeks, tugged her chin up to make her look at him. His Adam's apple jumped.

Eoin was completely awake now, and she wanted to melt into the bed.

Idiot.

"I dinnae mean ta hurt ye, Ash." His voice was low, sincere.

Use of her nickname didn't stop the rush of honesty. "Well, you did. You were all hot and heavy, kissing me all over the place, holding me, then nothing. Pushing me away like a leper." She shrugged. Tears welled against her will, and Ashlyn called herself every name in the book. *Again.*

She'd rejected *him*; she had no right to accuse him of the reverse. Eoin was going to think she was fickle. Or worse, unstable.

"Oh, lass." He sounded pained, and his expression was a mix of surprise and regret. Eoin's eyes bored into hers. He didn't release his hold on her face, and thumbed away her tears as they were born. "I thought 'twas wha' ye wanted."

"It was. Then it wasn't."

Oh, God, he's really going to think I lost it.

"Eoin, I..." Ashlyn's words dried up. She swallowed, but it didn't help.

He caressed her cheek, and she couldn't pull away.

"I dinnae mean ta hurt ye," he repeated.

Their gazes collided.

If her mouth was dry before, it was a desert now. Ashlyn's body thrummed for him, begging in ways she couldn't voice.

Eoin seemed to get it. His eyes went from sapphire to stormy, to midnight-at-sea.

Her tongue was glued to the roof of her mouth. She tried not to fidget away from that unwavering, yet impossibly gentle touch still against her cheeks.

It wasn't a tight grip; why couldn't she move?

His lips parted and Ashlyn felt her own answer that call. She tilted her chin up, asking.

His mouth came down, claiming hers.

She moved into him, slipping her arms around him, and pressing her breasts to his bare chest. The soft fabric of the sleeping gown didn't let her get close enough.

Ashlyn wanted it gone. Wanted to be naked in his arms. She shifted; the chemise restricted the movement, made her more aware of the separation between them, and she burned. Her sex throbbed. She ordered her brain to shut off. No matter what happened, she needed this right now. Needed him.

Maybe she had from the first time Eoin had kissed her outside the pub in Inverness.

He groaned and buried his hand in the hair at the back of her neck, pulling her closer still. He shoved his tongue in her mouth, rubbing it against hers, tasting her in a tangle of nips and licks as they both fought to kiss harder, deeper. "Lass," Eoin breathed against her lips. "I want ye. I need ye. I *need* ye, Ash."

Ashlyn leaned back. He'd called her *Ash* again, but it was still delicious in the way it rolled off his brogue. "I kinda thought that's what this was about. What I was trying to tell you."

Eoin stilled. Studied her, but Ashlyn did the same, scanning his gorgeous face, stubbled cheeks. The roughness against her skin made her want him more. His lips were swollen from hers, his complexion ruddy, and his massive chest heaved with his attempts to get control of himself.

She didn't want him controlled.

Ashlyn wanted *all* of Eoin MacLeod.

"Ye...ye...need ta be *certain*, lass. I dinnae let ye go easily."

I don't want you to.

Ashlyn couldn't say that aloud. It wasn't true.

Was it?

How could she have become so fond of this big Highlander in just a few days?

Fate? Like Angus said?

"I'm sure I want you," she whispered.

Eoin's answer was another searing kiss and he started tugging at the nightgown, moving his lower body into hers. His erection hit her in the right place, but there was still material separating them.

When her chemise was around her waist, his hot hands branded her hips and thighs.

She moaned. He was so close to where she needed

his fingers.

"Off. This needs off ye," Eoin breathed, pulling harder on the chemise.

"Don't rip it. I'll take it off." Ashlyn regretted having to sever their physical contact, even if it was only for a few seconds.

He took the same moment to rid himself of the shorts, and she couldn't help but stare at his erection.

She'd seen it before, felt it against her more times than that, but this time…it was going to be hers.

Eoin was going to be hers.

Tremors started in her spine and spread to her limbs; even her hands shook.

"Lass," he breathed. "Dinnae make me wait. I dinnae bear waitin' fer ye." His gaze ate her up.

She'd always been self-conscious, like any normal woman, but she couldn't be right then. Eoin's eyes declared her a goddess. Ashlyn's nerve endings responded to the visual call, and she tingled all over. The way he was looking at her was as good as a caress, but it wasn't enough. She needed his hands and mouth on her. All over her.

"No…waiting," she panted.

He made a guttural noise in his throat, and grabbed her shoulders, then possessed her mouth again. He kissed her into oblivion, leaving her a writhing, begging mess in his arms.

Eoin gently pushed her to the mattress, covering her body with his. His heated skin against hers revved her even higher. There was nothing between them, and feeling *all* of him against her was glorious. Better than in the cave when he'd kissed her awake.

Ashlyn cried out when he spread kisses downward, tracing her areolas with his tongue. Her nipples ached, they were so tight, and her sex throbbed in time with his teases.

His hands followed, cupping her before journeying on, and when Eoin crossed the soft part of her belly with seeking fingers, she trembled. Wanted to shove him away from the part of her body she didn't like in the mirror. Then he went lower and pressed his thumb into her clit.

Ashlyn screamed his name and threw her head back into the pillows, crushing her eyes shut as Eoin worked magic at her core. Her head thrashed but she couldn't stop; the sensations assailing her took all of her attention. Coherent thought fled.

He trailed kisses from one hip to another, before licking his way down her pelvis. "I need ta taste ye, Ash," he whispered.

The words enflamed Ashlyn and her thighs vibrated of their own accord even before he laved her sex from top to bottom. "Oh, God," she moaned.

He tormented her, kissing and nibbling everywhere but where she needed his mouth.

She whimpered, then he chuckled and did it again.

"You…tease."

Eoin flashed a wicked grin and nipped her inner thigh. "So wet fer me, already. An' ye taste like honey."

She bit her bottom lip to keep from crying out when he probed her opening with a gentle fingertip. Then he drove forward to his knuckles and sucked her clit into his mouth.

Ashlyn hollered his name and buried her hands in his hair. Her hips lifted of their own accord and she came hard, panting to stave off blackened vision. She shook from head to foot. Pleasure washed over her with every stroke of his fingers and tongue, until she was almost too sensitive.

Then Eoin was there, pulling her into his arms and holding her close, kissing her tenderly. She could taste her essence, and it zinged renewed desire over her limbs.

"More, Eoin. I need you inside me," she begged, rocking her hips into his.

"Aye, lass." His voice was so deep it was almost unrecognizable. He grunted and guided his erection to her sex. Eoin surged back to her, joining them in a hard thrust that pulled a long moan from Ashlyn.

She tugged his hair when he stilled above her.

"Did I hurt ye?" The veins in his neck stood out, as if he was holding himself back by the barest thread.

She shook her head. "No. No. Kiss me and move. I need you to move."

"Gladly." He pushed his pelvis against hers as he did her bidding, sealing his mouth over hers.

Every thrust made her soar higher. Ashlyn clung to Eoin, first with her arms around his neck, then gripping his biceps when his pistoning lost rhythm and she could only hold on. Sweat blanketed them both, but she didn't care.

Orgasm started to build and retreat with his movements, driving her crazy.

The faster he went, the harder he kissed her, until she saw stars. Ashlyn kept up, moving under him, with him.

She finally tugged away from their latest lip-lock when her muscles constricted. She jerked and ecstasy slammed into her. She gripped his arms because she needed to hold on to something.

Eoin grunted and stiffened above her as he came inside her, then he buried his face in her neck, his big body shuddering.

Gooseflesh peppered Ashlyn's body as her sex contracted, milking his, and her belly warmed with the rush of release.

"Jesu, lass," Eoin murmured against her overheated skin. When he lifted his head and met her gaze, his eyes were heavy-lidded and sated.

I did this to him.

Ashlyn kissed him because she didn't know what to say. Didn't know how to express how he'd just made her feel.

The romance writer. Speechless after sex.

It was for the best, probably. So, she wouldn't

blurt something like, *'this is the kind of sex I write about.'*

Because it *was.*

Eoin took over the kiss and held her tight even as he slipped from her body.

Their mouths slanted again, languorous, and heated, until Ashlyn's already boneless form melded into his chest on a sigh he swallowed.

"Ashlyn," he whispered. "Ashlyn. Yer…ye, lass. Yer…perfect."

She flushed and fought the urge to avert her eyes. "You're not so bad yourself." She missed the mark on her attempt at humor. Her voice was too thick, a croak.

Ashlyn had never had sex with someone she didn't love.

Then again, *this* hadn't felt like just sex.

Had Eoin made love to her?

She didn't love him…but she cared for him. *Could* love him.

Ashlyn quaked.

I can't love him. I have to go home.

"Are ye…okay, as ye say?" His brogue rolled over her, and she smiled at his use of the modern word.

She swallowed and nodded. "Aye."

The grin Eoin presented her with was lopsided and made her insides wobble.

"We traded words," she whispered.

"We traded more an' words, lass." He brushed his mouth over hers, but the tender gesture didn't shake the dread from settling low in her belly.

Not because she regretted giving herself to him. She didn't. Would do it again and would likely get the chance.

Could her heart handle the fallout?

Ashlyn still had to walk away from him in the end.

chapter fourteen

The sweet lass curled into his side made a noise in her sleep and Eoin nestled her closer. Ashlyn's arm was thrown across his middle as if she owned him, but he didn't mind. He liked the idea, actually. It felt right.

Is this my fate?

He'd taken her twice and would've made it thrice had she not kept yawning after shattering in his arms the second time.

God's Blood, she was perfect.

He'd been reckless with her, releasing his seed inside her, but he'd lost control. Panic should be greeting him now; Eoin could've put a child on Ashlyn tonight, but the thought didn't petrify him. It filled him with longing.

That should be alarming, too. Like nothing he'd felt before. Nothing he'd ever wanted.

He watched the rise and fall of her breasts as she slept in his arms.

Contentment to match the peaceful repose on her beautiful visage settled over him, as well as a fierce protectiveness.

How the hell was he going to let her walk away?

I made her a vow.

"I've no choice," Eoin whispered.

Ashlyn stirred and her long lashes fluttered as she came around. "Eoin?" She took a breath that brushed her nipples against his side. Her legs rubbed his thigh as she stretched and pushed her golden locks out of her face.

His cock jumped and he had difficulty concentrating, but he forced his eyes to hers. "Sorry ta wake ye."

She smirked. "It's not like we got much sleep anyway." Even in the dimness of his rooms, he could see the crimson tinge to her cheeks.

Eoin laughed. "Shall I apologize again?"

She shook her head, and her hair danced, teasing his bare skin. Ashlyn propped her torso on his chest, the softness of her flawless breasts pressing ever closer; his shaft tingled as blood filled it.

He'd be granite in seconds, and she hadn't even touched him there.

"I'm gonna be yawning until noon. Angus is going to wonder why I'm so tired."

He chuckled. "My grandfa's been 'round a long time. I think he'll suspicion." He caressed her cheek, smiling when she kissed his palm.

"That doesn't make me feel better," Ashlyn whispered.

"Why, lass?"

"Not sure I want him to know what we've been

up to."

"Fair enough." He thumbed her cheekbone and his Ashlyn leaned into the touch.

She rested her hand on the outside of his and tilted her head. "I guess it was worth the no-sleep thing."

"Ye *guess*? Dinnae be certain?"

Her grin was wicked, and she shook her head again.

Eoin growled and tugged her down to him, taking her mouth roughly, answering her dare. "Ye play wit' fire, lass." He pushed the statement into her lips.

"Then burn me."

Tremors danced down his limbs when she slid her leg over him, straddling his hips. Her naked sex brushed his and his erection stood at attention, throbbing a demand.

Ashlyn dragged her hands, then her breasts down his chest and he hissed.

"Vixen."

She giggled.

The soft curve of her bottom compressed his cock against his inner thigh, and his bollocks prickled. He gripped her waist when she started rocking her pelvis into his. The sensation was too much and not enough. "Lass." It was supposed to be a demand but came out a whispered plea.

His Ashlyn was making him beg.

She licked her lips and leaned down, pressing a small kiss to his mouth that was also not nearly enough.

Eoin pushed his hands up her slender back, mapping every inch of her supple flesh.

She whimpered and dipped down for another kiss.

He fused his mouth to hers, pinning her to him with one hand on her neck and the other claiming the small of her back. Their tongues danced, dueled for dominance, until she pulled away with a pant.

"You were supposed to burn me." Her dark eyes were pools of midnight, and her gorgeous face was flushed pink, her freckles standing out in stark contrast. Her lips were swollen from his and parted just enough to make him want to taste her again.

"Yer in control. Ye mounted me," he breathed.

Desire flared in her gaze and Ashlyn ground against him. "You're right. I'm going to take what I want."

Eoin groaned and pushed his head back into the plush feathers of his pillow.

She undulated but didn't put him inside her.

"Yer tryin' ta kill me."

A delighted laugh rolled over him and he smiled, but closed his eyes and breathed deeply, so his vision would stop dancing.

She teased him some more, kissing his neck and nibbling his chin, then pressed a scorching kiss to his mouth before moving on, laving her tongue down his chest.

His spine tingled as if he would orgasm, and his bollocks pulsed. He was going to explode before he got inside her. "Lass, I dinnae survive a wait."

Ashlyn grabbed his hand and trailed his fingertips over her breasts, teasing her erect nipples, and moving down her belly. When she parted her folds with his fingers, they both moaned.

"Yer so wet. Take me, lass."

Finally, *finally,* she gripped and guided his erection to her sex. With every inch she sank down, Eoin's thoughts scattered, and pleasure washed over him. Her body gripped his better than his favorite gauntlets. Hot, and so wet. Sweet, and all his.

When her bottom hit his thighs, he grabbed her hips and helped her thrust until they fell into a natural rhythm. She planted her hands on his chest for leverage and the pressure took his breath, but he didn't care. She was riding him hard, rocking, thrusting, driving them higher and higher. His blood sang in his ears, well on its way to boiling over.

Ashlyn cried out, arching her back and closing her eyes. She tossed her head, making her hair fly wild and free, like the expression on her face as she climaxed. Her core squeezed his cock, giving him the last push before throwing him over the edge.

Eoin shuddered and lifted her, only to slam her pelvis into his as his release shot deep and his muscles went taut with each jerk inside her.

Air was scarce and his skin was too hot. He

panted to force breath into his lungs, but the condition was echoed in his lass. Her breasts heaved as Ashlyn came down and the image would be etched into his head for the rest of his days.

Her bare form shimmered in the dim light, covered in a sheen of sweat he wanted to lick off every inch of her. She was flushed a delicious pink from head to foot, a mix of vixen and innocent that drove him wild.

Ashlyn planted a hand on his abdominal muscles, and he caught the other one, bringing her knuckles to his mouth to press kisses there.

She was shaking from exertion, and he grabbed her slender biceps to help her slip off him and lie down. She gazed up at him as soon as her shoulders hit the linens. Her pretty eyes were half-mast and satisfied.

He hovered above her and lowered his mouth to hers. Eoin had to taste her again.

Words wouldn't form, so he couldn't tell her how beautiful she was when she let go like that, or how she'd made him feel.

Ashlyn had marked him. *Branded* him so he'd never want another woman.

When she walked away, she was going to leave him *ruined.*

A little voice whispered she was going to take his heart, but he ignored it. Pushed it away, refusing to examine what it could — what it *did* — mean.

"Eoin, what's wrong?"

"Nothin', lass. Ye take my breath away."

Truth.

That was as far as he could go with it. Eoin had made a vow and he'd see it through.

"You do the same to me." Ashlyn kissed him again, a tiny tender thing that made him smile. She nestled close, resting her hand over his pounding heart and her head on his shoulder.

"Pleases me ta hear tha'," he whispered. He stroked her arm to her elbow, reveling in her soft skin. Eoin could touch every part of her every day and never tire of exploring her, memorizing her.

Therein lay the problem.

"I should try to get some sleep." Ashlyn yawned and snuggled closer. "Nessie and some of the girls are going to market, and Fiona wants to go. She wants me to go, too. I want to see *everything*."

"Oh?" Eoin lifted his head to look down at her, but she'd already closed her eyes.

"Yeah. Jamie's going, and some guards, I guess."

"Aye." He'd never let his sister go out without MacLeod men-at-arms, even if his steward and servants were to accompany her.

"Maybe I can...barter for something..." The statement was infused with sleep, and his Ashlyn drifted off before he could ask her how much coin she wanted to take.

In the morning, he'd mention to Jamie she was to

have anything she wished.

Eoin's heart skipped as he studied the lass he'd brought to his time against her will.

The lass who'd not only forgiven him, but had taken him into her arms, into her body, and made him *feel* in ways he never had with any other lover.

She'd only been in 1755 for days.

Too bad he couldn't remember a time before her and wasn't looking forward to *after* she'd left him.

Eoin swallowed the sorrow that rolled over him. It wasn't fair to demand of Ashlyn how much time he had left with her.

He'd promised her time at Dunvegan was in her control. When she requested to be taken home, he'd do so without delay, because of his vow.

Did he dare tell her he'd changed his mind?

Assert he couldn't let her go?

Nay, I cannot. I will not be an honorless bastard.

How would Eoin go on after Ashlyn left?

ashlyn looked up from the parchment full of her notes when the yelling started.

Angus paused mid-sentence. He'd been telling her more about the story of his parents' marriage, how his mother had come to the Human Realm and met his father by accident.

So far, she'd been fascinated by the Fae, except she didn't care for how they felt about humans—or those of mixed blood like Angus, Eoin, and Fiona, as well as some other close cousins.

Angus' poor mother had had to leave him with the MacLeods after his birth. He'd been with people who'd loved him, but the princess hadn't been able to join them to live until he was almost ten years old. She'd missed out on *years* of his life since she'd only been able to visit sporadically. His younger sister, Alexandria had been luckier; she'd been born after Alana had joined the clan permanently. Eoin's grandfather had not yet delved into his sister's story.

It made Ashlyn ache—the thought of a mother without her child. Especially a woman who was also away from her husband and they desperately loved each other. The hopeless romantic in her wanted to reject what'd happened.

The shouting got louder, and multiple voices now. Males other than Eoin.

"What the heck?" Ashlyn whispered, exchanging a look with the elderly man. She set the quill down, managing not to get ink on herself or her hands—a first, for sure. Learning to write with it had been a challenge.

Eoin had taught her how not to blot the ink, or have it drip and make her words illegible. He'd told her she had a neat hand, too.

She'd been in the eighteenth century for three weeks now and had been his lover for most of that time. She shivered.

Ashlyn was falling hard for the laird and had been trying to talk herself out of it since those feelings started to surface. But then again, they'd been there since day one, if she was honest.

Eoin yelled again and there was a feminine response. They were too far away to make out specifics down the hall in Angus' room, but the anger was clear.

Fiona.

"Oh no," she whispered, pushing to her feet at the same time the old man stood from his rocker.

He went to the window instead of the door. "Good. They're here."

"Who?" Ashlyn followed and spotted several horses clustered together in the bailey.

"The MacDonalds."

She did the math and gasped. "Eoin's gonna kill you."

Angus chuckled. "Nay. This needs ta be settled. He dinnae handle it."

"He won't let her marry him." So, her lover had told her over and over again when she'd asked about the almost-argument she'd witnessed the day she'd arrived, and after several other Fiona-Eoin shouting matches she'd witnessed since coming to 1755.

"We will see abou' tha'. My lassie loves tha lad. His surname should no' keep them apart. He's a fine, braw lad. Come, lass, we have a meetin'." Angus lifted his elbow, and Ashlyn slipped her hand onto his forearm, trying not to fidget at his side.

Eoin had been so staunch about his sister not marrying the boy she'd fallen for through clandestine trysts—although he surely didn't know when or how they'd spent time together. The laird was obviously angry, but she hoped his grandfather could prevent someone from getting hurt, as well as settle the matter, as he'd said.

There'd been peace between Clan MacLeod and Clan MacDonald for more than a hundred years. Her laird was being stubborn.

The girl had told Ashlyn she hadn't had sex with Kenneth, but the young couple had done some exploring of each other's bodies. If her brother found out, he'd either force them to marry—if the boy hadn't been a MacDonald—or kill him. Fiona was still technically a virgin, but Eoin wouldn't care.

Not that Ashlyn was about to share with the class. Fiona loved Kenneth, and she was all for them being together. Hopefully Angus could be the voice of reason.

They were so young, and marriage was forever, especially in this century, but it was also not unusual for teenagers to marry on this side of history.

She winced when they made it into the laird's solar — the lovely sunny and warm room where Eoin took assignations when he didn't want to share the privacy of his small ledger room.

He had a sword in his hand.

Jamie, his cousin, and Clan Steward, stood next to him, his eyes darting all over, face pale.

Fiona was on her feet, arms and legs spread out as she stood in front of a young redheaded man.

Kenneth MacDonald, Ashlyn could only assume. Like most Highlanders, he was tall and broad, so the petite girl protecting him could've been laughable, but she was smart.

Her brother was dangerous with a sword in his hand; Ashlyn had seen it firsthand when he'd sparred in the bailey.

The boy looked his age — he was only nineteen. He was clean shaven and handsome. Clad in a kilt with dark red as the base color, he had a sword belted on his waist. At least it wasn't drawn.

There was a well-dressed, dark-haired man

standing behind the boy, also wearing MacDonald plaid. He had a scroll in his hand and a scowl on his bearded face. His other palm was high in the air.

He'd probably just ordered the other two MacDonalds with them not to draw their swords, despite the fact the MacLeod laird was being aggressive. He had to be the Laird MacDonald, Kenneth's father, Callum.

Both the other men were also dark-haired and flanked their laird, hands on the hilts of their claymores. One guy was even bigger than Eoin, and frowning so hard his bushy eyebrows formed a unibrow.

"What 'tis this?" Angus boomed. Despite his advanced age, the demand carried, and all eyes shot to him.

"Grandfa!" Fiona cried, but she didn't move from her would-be betrothed.

Smart lass.

"The MacDonalds—" Eoin started at the same time.

"Enough!" Angus shouted.

Ashlyn slipped from his arm and stood right inside the room. She didn't really belong here, but Eoin's eyes found hers and his expression softened, if only for a second. When he looked away, he was all angry laird/overprotective big brother again.

Fiona was in tears and the young man behind her looked torn. He obviously wanted to comfort her, but was wary of Eoin.

Smart guy.

At least Ashlyn could see he loved the sweet girl she'd come to adore in her time at Dunvegan.

"Eoin-lad, stand down." This time, Angus' voice was softer, but a command, nonetheless.

The laird's frown deepened. "Angus—"

"*I* invited Laird MacDonald an' his heir ta discuss an alliance."

Eoin growled, but he sheathed the sword. He still looked pissed as hell, his broad shoulders stiff and his spine as straight as a board.

Ashlyn wanted to go to him, but what was her place here?

She wasn't his wife, so she shouldn't be at his side.

The truth singed her heart.

Callum MacDonald cleared his throat and stepped forward. "My steward prepared a marriage contract." His brogue was thick, but somehow refined. He was an educated man, and it piqued her interest.

Angus crossed the room and accepted the parchment, rolling it open to scan it.

Fiona's face lit up, which only made her brother glower more. She slid backwards and Kenneth entwined their fingers. The softness in her young expression—the hope and love for the boy beside her—made Ashlyn's heart skip, but she was envious too.

She spared Eoin a glance, but he was watching the

couple, disapproval stamped all over his face. Her tummy ached. She wanted him to look at her the way the boy was looking at his sister.

Kenneth's expression was the same as Fiona's, and Ashlyn tried to banish her jealousy.

Ashlyn slid to Eoin's side against her better judgment, and despite the tension in the room. "Eoin."

His sapphire gaze met hers. "Ashlyn-lass." At least his handsome face had lost most of the anger—only when he looked at her. He was still seething, and his big frame had a slight tremor he was obviously holding in check. For now.

He didn't reach for her, but Ashlyn couldn't help herself. She grabbed his hand and pushed her fingers through his.

Eoin didn't push her away—a good sign. He cradled her hand in his much larger one and pinned her to his side. Didn't smile, but his chest heaved as if he'd taken a breath, and he squared his shoulders. "Thank ye," he whispered, low enough for her ears only.

She'd been able to calm him.

Good.

The young couple also still holding hands didn't miss their interaction, and Fiona threw a grateful smile her way, which Ashlyn returned.

"This looks well enough ta me," Angus announced. "Fair. Eoin-lad, take a look."

Callum MacDonald gave a slight nod; his son

quirked a half-smile and squeezed Fiona's hand.

Eoin tugged free of Ashlyn's grip and snatched the parchment so fast she feared he ripped it.

He glared at his grandfather and sister, then all the MacDonalds. He grunted as he read, taking double the time Angus had, before rolling the thing back up and placing it in the elderly man's waiting hand. "I dinnae like it," he grumbled.

His sister scowled.

Kenneth MacDonald cleared his throat, and all eyes landed on the young man.

Fiona gasped when her heart's desire knelt before Eoin.

"Laird MacLeod," the boy said. "I'd like ta call ye brother. More than tha', I shall make yer sister happy. I...I love her." Sincere hazel eyes looked up at Ashlyn's lover, despite Eoin's hard expression.

She had an instant like of the kid. If she hadn't been rooting for them before, she certainly was now. He had balls to fight for what he wanted.

Eoin glowered.

Ashlyn sucked in a breath. She grabbed his forearm and tugged. She had no business doing what she was about to, but she loved Fiona, too.

Something declared the girl wasn't the only MacLeod she felt that way about, but she shoved it to the back of her mind. "Eoin," she whispered when he didn't look at her right away. Ashlyn pulled harder.

He swung those blue eyes to hers but didn't

speak.

"Can't you see how badly they want this? How much they love each other? Angus can see it. Laird MacDonald can see it. Can you not?"

Eoin stared down at her. Silent. Stoic. However, not frowning.

Is it good or bad?

Ashlyn held her breath and suspected she wasn't the only one doing so in the room.

The tension was so thick it was almost visible.

Her lover's Adam's apple bobbed, then his gaze landed on his sister and the young man with his knees still to the stone. "Get up," Eoin barked.

The boy obeyed, but he didn't hang his head. He met Eoin's gaze dead on, which shot Ashlyn's admiration of him up a few notches.

Fiona knows how to pick 'em.

Eoin gently pulled out of Ashlyn's hold and stepped forward. He cupped his sister's face and appeared to look deep into her eyes. "'Tis what ye truly wan', lassie?"

A tear slid down Fiona's cheek, but she nodded. "Aye," the girl whispered. "More than anathin'."

He released a gust of air, but to his credit, Eoin no longer wore a scowl. He gave a curt nod and rejoined Ashlyn. "Verra well. We'll have a weddin'."

A murmur of approval rippled through Angus and the MacDonalds.

Fiona screeched and pounced on Ashlyn. The girl

wrapped her arms around her and squeezed almost too tight. "Thank ye, thank ye, thank ye," she chanted.

Ashlyn laughed and backed away, grabbing the teen's hands. "Thank your grandfather; he's always been your champion, and your brother, sweetie."

Eoin's sister shook her head and leaned in. "'Tis ye, Lady Ashlyn. *Ye*, and how my brother feels abou' ye." She planted a kiss on her cheek and flitted away.

Ashlyn flushed to her toes and tried to look anywhere but at Eoin.

He was looking back at her with emotion in those blue eyes.

She wanted to go to him, touch him, kiss him, but not with their audience.

Fiona was in Kenneth's arms and the laird turned a glare on them, but neither of the newly betrothed was bothered—or seemed to notice anyone else in the room.

Stuff like that made a girl believe love could solve the world's problems. Ashlyn sighed and smiled, then called herself three kinds of stupid. Fiona was going to marry the man of her dreams, and *she* was going back to the future, leaving *hers* in 1755.

She startled.

Is Eoin the man of my dreams?

How could he be?

He was born three hundred years before she was.

They came from different worlds.

Literally.

Ashlyn's heart skipped and the answer she didn't want to face echoed in the back of her mind.

She'd fallen in love with Eoin MacLeod, and as feared, it was hopeless. Her stomach fluttered and a lump formed in her throat. She blinked back tears.

Laird MacDonald demanded his attention, as did his brother-in-law-to-be, and at least he seemed friendlier than he had before. Eoin shook the older man's hand, then Kenneth's.

Fiona practically bounced at the kid's side.

Angus was speaking in low tones to the other two MacDonalds and they all wore pleased expressions.

Sweat broke out on Ashlyn's brow. The walls seemed to be closing in on her, and she had to pant to breathe. Her head spun. The need to flee surfaced and overwhelmed.

No one would notice anyway, right?

She slipped from the room. Her vision blurred before she got halfway down the hall to the lady's suite. Rooms she hadn't spent much time in since she'd been sleeping with Eoin.

Ashlyn shut the door with a slam she'd not intended and collapsed on top of the quilt his mother had made. The sob rose up and took over, wracking her frame.

She stuck her face in the pillow to muffle the noise. Hugged a smaller, cylindrical, tasseled one to her chest so tight she couldn't breathe. The navy-blue corset bit into her sides, but she didn't adjust her position.

Ashlyn was so happy for Fiona and Kenneth, but so sad for her and Eoin.

Of course, she'd known they were doomed. They couldn't have a real relationship; she had to go home.

She loved him anyway.

What am I going to do?

chapter sixteen

h e looked up and she was gone. Eoin's gut shouted to go after her, but his soon-to-be family by marriage was demanding his attention. Making inquiries about things he'd rather not discuss with MacDonalds, impending marriage or not.

Why the hell had he agreed to this?

He studied the lad his little pest longed to call husband. Kenneth was young—only nine and ten, but the lad was braw. Matched his height. His muscle was leaner but given a few years to fill out the lad would match his bulk as well.

The emotion on the MacDonald heir's face might highlight his youth, but it stirred something in Eoin. Not for his sister, but for…Ashlyn.

Her dark eyes, pleading and sincere for Fiona's marriage, had cinched it for him—or at least convinced him what his sibling wanted was genuine.

The lad had done the rest, declaring first he'd wanted to call him brother. Kenneth MacDonald had only said what he'd thought Eoin wanted to hear.

He'd been wrong. The most important part of his speech had been how he'd ended it—confessing his love for Fiona.

Eoin grunted and narrowed his eyes. "I'll kill ye if ye dinnae take care a' her. Keep her *happy*."

"Aye, my laird," the lad replied without missing a beat.

"I'll be happy, brother." His sister's face lit up.

He'd never seen her so joyful. Fiona's eyes shone for the redheaded lad. She was hanging on his arm, too.

His gut ached. Again, his Ashlyn's absence took front and center. The bright room was dim without her. Cold, too.

Where had she gone?

Why had she gone?

She'd been the reason he'd relented. She had to know that.

"Jamie's my head steward; he can answer ta yer concerns," he told Laird MacDonald and gestured to his cousin, who'd been hovering nearby.

The man bowed, and new conversation was born.

Eoin excused himself and whirled away. Needed to get to his Ashlyn.

His grandfather's weathered hand appeared on his forearm. "Let her go, lad. Tha lass looked as if she needed some time."

"Why?"

"Let us go ta my room an' speak. The need fer yer presence here, 'tis done."

Eoin nodded and threw one last look to his sister.

Fiona was still glowing at the lad's side, hanging

on his arm while he and his father talked to their cousin.

His gut tightened. He was giving her away. However, he believed the lad's feelings and intentions were sincere.

"All is well here. 'Tis settled," Angus remarked, following his gaze.

Eoin was still angry at his grandfather for the ambush. *He* was Laird MacLeod, not Angus, but seeing his little pest so elated had softened his ire, if only a bit.

He followed the elderly man to his rooms and took the seat by the hearth, opposite the rocking chair, when bid. Words tumbled out without delay. "I vowed I'd return her ta her time."

"Aye, she tol' me."

As if compelled, the truth fell from his lips. "I dinnae be able ta let her go, Grandfa." He wanted to avoid that shrewd blue gaze, but his eyes found Angus' of their own accord.

"Then dinnae." The man rocked forward in his chair, his tone casual, belying his expression.

"She dinnae be willin' ta stay…"

"I ken it."

Eoin jolted. "Ye ken…?"

Angus nodded. "I dinnae think yer fate…'tis ta remain here fer tha rest a' yer days."

He swallowed. Wanted to demand so much about this sudden revelation, but nothing would come out of his mouth. Eoin fidgeted and stared at the man who'd raised him.

"Ye dinnae be the first MacLeod ta share such a future fate. I knew yer's when ye were wee, Eoin-lad. The Stones dinnae just call ta ye. They sing in yer blood. 'Tis why ye belonged travelin' all this time. Ye can settle, ken yer supposed ta be in tha future. Mayhap 'tis why ye met tha witch in tha first place. She taught ye of things ye needed ta know. 'Tis fate, too."

A part of his grandfather's magic was premonitions or visions, but the fact that the old man had known such a belief for *years* and kept it from Eoin, made him more than speechless. His insides wobbled, and he had to inhale a few times before he could speak. "My magic—"

"'Tis stronger than my own when it comes ta tha Faery Stones."

Shock rolled over him and he blinked. He pitched his body forward in the chair. His shoulders, his back, even his thighs were clenched to the point of pain, and Eoin couldn't keep his leg from jumping. "I'm tha laird. I've a duty ta my clan."

"There are many MacLeods, lad, but only one lass callin' ta yer heart."

Emotion clogged in his throat, and he had to look away before he could meet his grandfather's eyes again. He couldn't make sense of the chaos swirling in his head.

Could he even consider what his grandfather was declaring?

Eoin would have to name an heir. Angus was two and ninety. Although he was hale, they didn't know how many years he had left, and Eoin couldn't place the burden of the clan on his shoulders yet again.

"Grandfa—"

"Ye need no' fash, lad. Go ta tha future wit' yer lass. Live yer life by her side. Sweet Ashlyn dinnae want ta let *ye* go, either."

He jumped. "Did she say so? Ta ye?" The questions had a demanding edge that made the old man chuckle.

"Nay, foolish lad. 'Tis no secret how she looks a' ye. Or how ye look a' her."

Warmth flushed to Eoin's toes. He couldn't confirm or deny his feelings. His heart picked up speed and he hoped—prayed—with his whole being, his soul, Angus spoke the truth. "She dinnae say—" he whispered.

"Have ye?"

Eoin shook his head on instinct, even though this was the last subject he'd ever thought he'd discuss with the elderly man. It was bad enough when Angus was too perceptive. Confessing…feelings…made him feel like an errant lad being admonished.

His grandfather *tsked* like a nagging woman. "Then yer both foolish."

He let the chide slide, desperate for a distraction. "I need ta sit fer tha' paintin'."

"Aye, a' fore ye go, ye do. Call fer an artist on tha

morrow. Looks like tha work a' Sulwen MacInnes. At least he's here on Skye."

"An' tha Flag?"

"'Twill call ta a new guardian if an' when 'tis necessary."

"I'll have ta name an heir."

"Aye, ye will." Angus reclined in his chair only to rock forward again, the curved wooden tines giving a creak as he had an answer for Eoin's every concern.

That had irritated him since he was wee, but at the same time, he loved the man for the ability. His grandfather had calmed him.

I should thank him.

"Fiona…" His voice failed him again. He'd miss his little pest if he were to proceed with this madness.

If Ashlyn would even have him.

"Will be taken care a', as always." His grandfather smiled softly. "She's ta be wed now, ta tha man a' her choice. Kenneth MacDonald will be good ta tha lassie. He loves her, an' she loves him. They should be tagether. Like ye an' Ashlyn-lass."

"Grandfa—"

Angus planted his feet to the floor and leaned forward, making a grab for his forearm. "I ken, Eoin-lad. I ken it." He squeezed, and his smile widened. "My Lila came ta me. Ye need ta go ta yer Ashlyn, an' ken yer family, yer clan, will be hale, because yer where…*when*…yer supposed ta be."

Eoin didn't know what to say, so he just nodded.

The lump in his throat didn't dissipate, no matter how many times he swallowed against it.

He had a lot to think about.

chapter seventeen

The day the contract was signed the wedding was planned for two days hence, and Fiona was to wear the ivory gown her mother had worn to marry her father.

Today's her big day.

The chapel on Dunvegan's grounds was larger than the one the MacDonalds' had at Armadale, so they'd agreed to hold the wedding on Clan MacLeod lands. They'd all return within the hour, and no doubt would bring the whole clan.

Father Percival had already arrived, although Eoin had grumbled that he was a Sassenach. He looked like a nice enough guy to Ashlyn. He was short and stout with naturally rosy cheeks that gave him a cheery appearance. His thinning hair was blond and his smile easy. It wasn't the poor guy's fault he'd been born English.

A huge feast was planned for after the ceremony, and Eoin wanted to outdo his former rivals, which had Jamie pulling his hair out. Huge shipments of food had been arriving for two days.

Nessie and her girls had done several dress fittings for Fiona, at Cinderella-mouse-speed to get the alterations done. They'd also had Dunvegan decorated at a supernatural pace, making Ashlyn suspect the housekeeper had magical powers, too. Her abilities didn't seem human.

"Oh, sweetie, you look gorgeous," Ashlyn whispered as she surveyed the beautiful, intricately beaded dress on Fiona's perfect petite figure.

The neckline was modest, but somehow fitting, and the pearled pattern over the bodice must've taken some poor seamstress forever. It had puffy sleeves and yards of fabric flowing to the floor with a pretty lacy overlay that would make Kate jealous.

Eoin's sister had insisted she be there when she dressed, and Ashlyn couldn't refuse. She'd told them all she'd help however she could.

"Thank ye." The bride-to-be twirled, beaming, her dimple a beacon to her happiness.

The large mirror sat at-the-ready, and Fiona faced it, studying her reflection. Her cheeks were bright, and her ebony locks had been braided up, with pink and white flowers woven in, like a natural tiara.

She was so lovely it was going to take Kenneth's breath away.

It was a good thing Ashlyn's own attire was again green, but this time a darker hue. Her eyes might as well have been the same color, she was so jealous of her lover's sister.

She could taste the envy, it was so thick, and even though that made her feel guilty as hell, she couldn't seem to shake it.

Unfortunately, it ruined Ashlyn's ability to appreciate the pretty gown Maegan had found for her to wear, too. It wasn't as fine as the bride's, of course, but it had tiny little silver flowers sewn into the sheer long sleeves, and along the low neckline. Like Fiona's green dress, it gave Ashlyn awesome cleavage, and the corseted bodice made her waist look tiny.

Maybe Kate was on to something with the corset thing.

Her bestie's smile floated into her head, making Ashlyn sigh. She missed Kate but had to admit since she'd started sleeping with Eoin, she'd rarely worried about what was going on in the future.

Great, 'cause yeah, I need more guilt.

Kate would probably be frantic by now. It'd been over three weeks. Then again, did time pass the same here and there?

Ashlyn frowned.

"Somethin' wrong, Ash?" Fiona asked.

She jerked. Forced a smile. "No, of course not."

The girl had taken to using her nickname, too. She preferred when her brother said it, despite the similar charming brogue.

"Do ye like my hair? How does it look? Peg and Maegan did it fer me."

"You're flawless, honey. Kenneth's going to faint when he sees you."

Fiona grinned and shook her head. "I hope he

dinnae."

"It'll be perfect, kiddo. No worries."

She let out an audible breath and seemed to look over Ashlyn for the first time. "Yer bonnie, as well. My brother will love ye in tha' gown."

Ashlyn's heart skipped. Eoin and *love*…in the same sentence was too much to hope for. "Are you ready to go down?" she managed. Needed a distraction.

The girl's blue eyes darted around the room as if she expected to be ambushed at any moment, even though they were alone. Nessie had stepped out when Ashlyn arrived.

"May I ask ye somethin'?"

"Sure, what's up?"

Fiona stepped forward and grabbed her hand. "I need ta know…" Her alabaster complexion flamed red to her ears, and it dawned on her what the girl was trying to say.

"Wedding night jitters?"

She nodded. "I tried ta ask Nessie, but she dinnae tell me. Dinnae be proper, she said. When I was a lassie, she dinnae even talk ta me about my bleedin' 'til it started."

Of course, she wouldn't discuss it.

Ashlyn fought her irritation at the well-meaning but ridiculous housekeeper. Womanly secrets shouldn't be kept from other *women*. "Tell me what you…know."

Fiona averted her gaze and shifted on her feet. "Kissin' is...good." Her cheeks lit up even rosier. "Kenneth has touched me...down there. I've touched him, as well..."

Ashlyn's tummy fluttered. Why did *she* have to get stuck with the sex-ed lesson?

She sucked back a sigh.

You adore this girl, that's why.

It was 1755, and as proven by Nessie's refusal, this kind of thing just wasn't discussed. Fiona deserved to be told what sex with her husband would be like.

"Do you know the mechanics of sex...intercourse?"

Their eyes met, and the girl nodded. "Aye. The lad goes inta tha lass."

"Right. And you've never done that before?"

Fiona shook her head.

"Okay." Ashlyn blew out a breath. "The first time will...hurt. You may bleed afterward, but the more you do it, the better it'll feel, and there won't be pain. Only pleasure."

The girl's eyes widened with her every word. "Kenneth would ne'er hurt me."

"He won't do it on purpose, sweetie. The first time for a woman...just hurts."

"What abou' tha first time fer a lad?"

"Kenneth's a virgin?" Ashlyn didn't mean to sound so surprised—and she did, even to her own ears—but when Fiona nodded, she liked the kid even more. "The good news is your first time won't likely last too long, so hopefully it won't hurt too much." She groaned when Fiona asked what that meant.

She kept firing questions, and Ashlyn did her best to be open and honest. Fiona knew babies resulted from, *'lovin','* as she'd termed it, and the girl revealed she also knew what happened when a man orgasmed.

Eoin would've killed Kenneth on the spot.

She was open in what they'd done together, and had also had an orgasm, although she hadn't known what it was called until Ashlyn told her.

Even though it was all for educational purposes, talking about sex made her obsess over how Eoin touched and kissed her, how he moved inside her, and what it felt like when *she* climaxed. Desire teased below the surface of her skin and Ashlyn squeezed her thighs tight, glad her gown was full.

She tried not to fidget, and reminded herself the conversation was about Fiona and Kenneth, not her and her laird. "Believe me, when you get the hang of it, sex is awesome, and you'll learn to please each other without effort."

"I want tha'. I love him," Fiona whispered, her expression soft and sweet.

"I know, and that makes all the difference."

"'Tis like tha' fer ye an' my brother, dinnae?"

Ashlyn flushed to her toes and swallowed.

It is for me.

She couldn't say it; even though she was confident

her conversation with his sister was under a cone of silence. Plus, she didn't really want to admit she and Eoin were lovers; they weren't married.

It was wrong in the majority of eighteenth-century eyes, even though men could sleep around as much as they wanted.

Women could not.

Hypocrites.

One of the many plights of being a woman in the past. Which was why it was better in books, of course.

Ashlyn never suppressed her heroines. She always wrote strong women, like her and Kate. Although, when it came to Eoin, she didn't feel so strong.

"Ye love my brother."

Her head nodded of its own accord, and she cursed. When she finally had the guts to look at Fiona, the girl was beaming.

"I ken it ta be true. He loves ye, too." She darted forward and wrapped her arms around Ashlyn.

Ashlyn hugged her back, blinking tears away she didn't want her to see. She didn't have the heart to contradict her, since Fiona had looked so happy about it. Nor could she acknowledge how her whole body lit up at the prospect.

It didn't matter.

Even if Ashlyn was lucky enough for Eoin to love her, the result would be the same as if he didn't.

Her heart shattered into a million pieces the day

he brought her home.

His little pest was so gorgeous she glowed with it. Actual radiance, as if shining from her skin. Evidently, she was so excited to exchange vows, Fiona couldn't seem to be solemn in front of the Sassenach priest. She fairly bounced as she stood next to Kenneth MacDonald, her arm looped in the lad's.

Not proper at all, and yet it made Eoin want to grin, despite the subtle noises of disapproval Nessie was making from the second row of seats in the MacLeod chapel. The housekeeper would *have to deal,* as Ashlyn would say.

His lover stood by his side, staring at the young couple with an unreadable expression.

He'd expected her to smile, in the very least, but she was stoic.

Was she upset about something?

She'd pressed for this wedding, after all. Seeing his sister happy had made it all worth it.

Eoin studied Ashlyn's profile. His lover. His love, although he'd never called her such aloud. He really should.

I love her.

Emotion smacked him in the face, and he shifted in his boots. He *did* love the lass from the future. Angus' words haunted him, and he pushed them away. Tried to focus on the *now.* Ashlyn at his side, with her slender hands on the back of the pew in front of her as she stood to witness the wedding.

She was breathtaking in the dark green gown, and her breasts were displayed prominently enough that he wanted to growl at all his kinsmen—not to mention the MacDonalds present—if they dared to look at her.

Her hair was loose today, falling in thick waves down her back, and he wanted to sweep the golden locks off her shoulders to lay a line of kisses along her neck. Perhaps taste the soft skin behind the shell of her ear, too.

How was Eoin going to survive hours upon hours of a wedding feast without covering her up, or worse—having to keep his hands to himself?

As laird, it wasn't likely he'd be able to sneak to his rooms early with her. He had to be a proper host, especially since his guests were Clan MacDonald. He'd be stuck in the hall all evening. Watching Ashlyn and unable to have her.

Eoin swallowed a gulp as his manhood twitched against the wool of his plaid. He needed to forget about making love to Ashlyn for now and concentrate on his sister exchanging vows with the lad she loved.

He'd have *his* love all to himself later that night, when they retired—even if it'd be much later than he'd like.

Kenneth took Fiona's fingers in his as the Sassenach instructed, then the priest wrapped a strip of MacDonald plaid around their joined hands. Both lad and lass repeated the vows as instructed, grinning at each other as if they were alone in the room.

His heart jumped, and Eoin imagined Ashlyn up on that dais, clad in his mother's dress. Her hand would be in his and the plaid wrapped around them would be MacLeod hues, not MacDonald.

With a silent curse, he shook the image away. He'd made her a vow.

Wouldn't break it.

That morning, Angus had asked if Eoin had made a decision about accompanying her to the future.

He hadn't.

Had he?

Hadn't talked to his lass about it, either, with all the wedding preparations of the last two days. Would she think him mad? Or would Ashlyn accept his love and agree they were fated?

His heart wanted one thing, but practicalities still needed to be handled. He'd not named an heir, but it would have to be his cousin Jamie, and Angus would approve.

Eoin had sat for the small painting yesterday.

Sulwen MacInnes had completed it in hours due to the size. If the renowned artist had thought the requested dimensions were unusual, he hadn't said. The image was now framed and mounted in his ledger room, next to a larger one of his father.

Eoin was ready, for the most part. Could he do it?

Walk away from his clan? His century?

For his Ashlyn?

He loved her. Did that change anything?

Aye.

That changed *everything.*

Clapping and joyful exclamations tugged him out of his head.

The ceremony was over, and the Sassenach priest announced his little pest was now someone's wife. Fiona MacDonald.

Eoin had missed the salute, but that was probably for the best. He'd not want instinct to run his new brother through to ruin the day.

Both newlyweds beamed, his sister's dimple on display as they faced their families, and Eoin couldn't help but feel proud that he and his grandfather had raised such a beauty. She'd never be demure, but she was gorgeous.

They looked at each other, a fleeting thing that melted into a stare, and the lad pulled Fiona to his side.

The move made Eoin's gut ache, for more than one reason.

He felt the same way about Ashlyn.

His little sister looked all grown up on the lad's arm, and Kenneth, too, looked older somehow than he had just days before in the solar where he'd begged for Fiona's hand.

Now he had it.

Poor wretch.

Eoin snorted.

"What is it?" Ashlyn asked.

He caught curiosity in her brown eyes and smirked. "Just occurred ta me, I dinnae warn tha lad what a handful my sister is."

His love grinned. "Oh well, they're married now. No takebacks."

He'd never heard the odd phrasing before, but he understood her meaning. The expression on her face was lighter than it'd been during the ceremony, and it stole his breath. He couldn't look away. Needed to touch her, too. "Are ye well, lass?"

"Of course. This is Fiona's day, and I'm so happy for her. Kenneth, too. They love each other." Something lurked in those deep brown eyes, but it was gone so fast he told himself he might've been seeing things.

Eoin caressed her cheek. "Well, my sister's a vision taday, no doub', but so are *ye*."

Ashlyn's cheeks brightened, but she didn't look away.

In the background, he was vaguely aware of the newlyweds leaving the chapel and both families starting to file out.

He didn't move. Stared at the lass who held his heart in her small hands. She didn't even know it. "Ashlyn—"

"We should go," she whispered. "Everyone's gone..."

Eoin tugged his eyes away from hers.

They were indeed alone.

How did that happen?

Even the Sassenach priest was nowhere to be found.

"The feast…"

"'Twill be there in moments." He gathered her close and dipped his head down, giving her a chance to slip away.

She didn't.

Ashlyn met his mouth and slid her arms around his waist. She squeezed him almost too tight and nestled into his chest. He rubbed his tongue against hers as she slanted her lips under his.

He plundered her, deepening the kiss as much as he could. She was so sweet, like the honey her hair always reminded Eoin of.

She tasted like that elsewhere, too.

Shudders of desire wracked him, and he tried to talk himself out of getting lost in the lass in his arms, but it was impossible. He caressed her lower back, moving downward, kneading her perfect bottom.

His cock was already hard, pitched into her stomach and he wanted to lift her to the back of the pew and push her gown around her hips so he could shove inside her.

Ashlyn rocked against him and pressed her breasts into his chest. She kissed him again, her mouth as hungry as his, and her grip on him tightened.

Eoin groaned when she nipped his bottom lip and

tugged away, contradictory to her encouragement moments before.

Her eyes were like the sea absent moonlight when their gazes locked, and she was panting, pushing her delectable breasts up in the square neckline.

He hollered at himself to look at her face.

She slipped from his arms, and it took all of his resolve to let her go. "We can't...we're in a chapel." Her cheeks were crimson, and when Ashlyn's eyes darted around the small sanctuary, it told him the condition wasn't only from arousal. "We can do this later."

Eoin growled and took her mouth in a quick hard kiss that only tempted him. Foolish on his part. "*Later* dinnae be now. 'Tis too far away."

Ashlyn swallowed and he wanted to kiss her throat. "I know. But this is *Fiona's* day." She straightened her gown and brushed her hands down the front of the full skirts.

"Are ye tryin' ta make me feel guilty?"

A smile played at the corner of her delicious mouth. She shook her head. "No, my laird. But your sister's not going to be here tomorrow. You'll miss her."

"Aye, I will." Eoin nodded. He sucked in much needed air and bid his blood to cool. His cock wasn't convinced. He needed a minute—or five—before he could go to the great hall with his lass on his arm. He'd rather retire to his rooms and make her scream his name.

Ashlyn reached to retie the lacing on the neckline of his leine and kissed his lips, then his chin. Soft brushes of her mouth that made him need more.

He chuckled and cupped her face. "That dinnae help, my lass." Endearments that were more, deeper, teased his palate, but he clamped down on them. For now. He'd tell her how he felt about her when the time was right. Eoin tried to convince himself he wasn't a coward.

"Help what? Your shirt was undone."

"An' I thank ye fer tha'. But yer mouth on mine certainly dinnae quench my desire ta take ye here. Now."

Her pretty eyes widened. "In the chapel? Eoin Alexander Duncan MacLeod."

He laughed again and planted a small kiss on her mouth; couldn't help it. He liked his full name on her lips. "Let us go ta tha hall." Eoin offered his arm to Ashlyn, and she slid her hand in his elbow.

"Will you dance with me?"

"Aye."

"Angus made me promise him a dance, too."

"He's tha only one," he growled.

She flashed a wicked grin. "Oh? Don't tell me you're jealous, my laird."

Eoin grumbled but gave into another chuckle when his Ashlyn laughed. Her whole countenance lit up and his heart skipped. He loved her so damn much and needed to tell her.

chapter eighteen

She stood by the window, rubbing her arm as she looked outside into the empty bailey. Ashlyn's eyes darted to the guarded gates of Dunvegan.

Fiona had been right there by those gates hours that felt like days ago. After her wedding, her new husband and his family had taken the girl to her new home, the MacDonald stronghold Armadale, on the other side of Skye.

Fiona had been so ecstatic. Had hugged her so hard and told Ashlyn to be happy with her brother.

Too bad she couldn't.

After the feast, Eoin had practically dragged her to his rooms. They'd been so eager for each other their clothing was still strewn all over the floor.

He'd made love to her so tenderly, worshipping her body, and with so much emotion in those sapphire eyes, she'd expected words that had never come.

That was for the better, or so Ashlyn had been trying to convince herself.

Eoin had looked like he'd wanted to say something a few times but hadn't. Each time, he'd kissed her instead, and she hadn't had the guts to explore her suspicions.

After he'd fallen asleep, Ashlyn had cried. She'd cried so hard it was a wonder she'd not woken him, but her laird had lain peacefully beside her. When she'd drifted off, she'd dreamt of home — the far future where he wouldn't be.

She'd woken with a start. It was early, and she'd drawn the drapes back in anticipation of watching the sun rise, but it hadn't just yet. Light was creeping slowly over the horizon as if afraid to make itself known. The in-between time when it wasn't light but wasn't night anymore. Fat white clouds made the sky a murky dark gray, hinting at morning rain. It was dreary, but that fit her mood perfectly.

Fiona's marriage had confirmed something she'd been avoiding.

It's time.

Ashlyn shivered. Probably should've put more clothing on than Eoin's leine. It fell mid-thigh but wasn't keeping her warm in the drafty castle. The fire had gone out sometime overnight. Her bare feet were already ice cubes on the stone floor, but she couldn't talk herself into getting back into that big bed with the man who'd stolen her heart.

"Ashlyn-lass?" Eoin called.

His soft voice shouldn't have startled her, but she jumped. Squeezed her eyes shut, too.

"Why're ye by the window? Dinnae ye be cold?"

The slap of his feet on the floor told her he'd

gotten up.

Eoin padded to her, then Ashlyn was enveloped in warmth—he'd put the plaid from his bed around her shoulders. It still held his body heat, and she wanted to burrow into it, and into him.

"It's time for me to go." She didn't turn and look at him. Couldn't. Should thank him for the blanket, but she couldn't do that, either.

"Go?"

The rustling of fabric told her he was pulling on a garment. "Home. To my time." Ashlyn stared out the window hard, as if the imminent sun could save her. Her heart was a brick in her stomach, and her *everything* hurt.

"Ashlyn—"

"I can't be here anymore." She sucked in a breath and held it. Ashlyn couldn't add that she couldn't be there with *him,* kiss him, make love to him, and not be able to *keep* him.

"I've been wantin' ta talk ta ye about tha'—"

Alarm washed over her, and she finally whirled to him. It'd taken her all night to work up the nerve to face going home. He'd better not ruin it. She *couldn't* stay. "What's to talk about? You promised. When I was ready. My terms, remember?"

"Aye." Eoin nodded and came closer, but she slid away. He was only wearing shorts, so he had to be cold, too.

If he touched her, it'd be bad. "I know a lot of

women in your family have come back in time and stayed…" Ashlyn's voice cracked, and she had to take another breath. "But I can't be like those other women, Eoin." Pain threatened to cripple her with the confession she'd never intended to say. It was the truth, which made it *worse*. She didn't want to look at him and see the hurt in his eyes, but she had to make her gaze meet his. "I…have to go back. My life is writing. My career. I finally made it. I can't live without it."

"I understand."

Ashlyn blinked. "Wh-what?"

He'd let her go like that?

Without a fight?

Isn't that what you wanted? You already reminded him of his promise. Idiot.

Wouldn't it make it easier if Eoin just agreed?

No.

Because it was already going to kill Ashlyn to walk away from him. It'd be worse if he was *okay* with the end of…them.

Eoin slid forward and cupped her face, stroking her cheekbones with his thumbs, wreaking havoc on her concentration. His sapphire eyes were impossibly soft.

She couldn't look away or ask him to stop touching her for her own sanity. She was compelled, as if by magic, to stand there.

"I'll go wit' ye."

Ashlyn startled, even in his gentle grip. "Wh-wh-what?"

"I want ye fer keeps, Ashlyn Elaine George."

She fought the urge to close her eyes as her whole name in his brogue destroyed her resolve to stay strong. Tears were born and scalded her cheeks. "I…"

"I've alreada spoken ta my grandfa. He agrees."

"But you have responsibilities here. To Angus. Fiona, too. She adores you even if she's married now. Your clan. You're the laird."

Eoin's smile made her belly flutter.

"I'm nothin' without ye, lass." This was low, but direct.

"I can't…let you walk away from your family." Ashlyn's voice wavered. She wanted to cling to him and demand his vow on what he was saying.

That's selfish.

"Ash, *mò gradh*, I'm *nothin'* without ye. No' a laird worth a damn. No' a man worth *anathin'*."

Mò gradh.

It meant *my love*, and Eoin had never called her that before.

Ashlyn's heart stumbled, and she tried to smile, but guilt swarmed. She wasn't willing to walk away from her career for him. A career, *not* a family. How could she let him leave his clan, his blood—not to mention he'd be stepping into the future, where he knew next to nothing about how to live.

"I love ye, lass."

The declaration was everything she'd always wanted, so why did Ashlyn feel like shit?

A sob rushed up and she covered her mouth. *Perfect,* ugly crying now, in front of the love of her life, when he'd confessed his feelings for the first time. "Eoin—" she choked out.

He guided them to the big bed and whispered sweet nothings in Gaelic, then wiped her tears away, and gathered her in to his chest as they sat.

Ashlyn buried her face against his neck because she didn't have the balls to look at him. She was going to have to tell him no and leave him in 1755.

Maybe even deny that she loved him, too.

How could she watch him open the Faery Stones and step through the portal *without* him?

She'd be weeping so hard she couldn't stand, let alone walk.

Ashlyn had no delusions about herself. She was a huge baby. A wimp. A girl who lived with her head in books.

Eoin rubbed her back and held her until she could get it together, because yeah, she needed another reminder of how awesome he was.

"I love you, too!" Ashlyn blurted. Then cursed herself to hell and back.

Why did you say that?

It would just make things harder.

"Look a' me, *mò gradh.*"

She couldn't have disobeyed even if she'd wanted

to. Tenderness and heat…and love swirled around in his gaze, and her heart shot into overdrive.

"My fate is wit' *ye*. My fate…'tis tha future."

Ashlyn swallowed. "I…I want to say yes. But I don't want you to resent me in a few years. What if—"

He put his fingertips to her lips. "I dinnae. I dinnae ever begrudge ye." Eoin wiped more tears away and smiled so big her insides combusted. "Ye…love me, *mò gradh*?"

"Well, of course, you big lug." She slapped his chest.

His chuckle washed over her and made Ashlyn smile through her tears.

Eoin caught her hand and kissed her knuckles, then pressed a hard fast kiss to her mouth. "I've thought abou' it, lass. My decision is final. I'll go with ye. I need ta. I want ta. Yer my fate."

"You're my fate?" Ashlyn whispered.

"Aye."

"Angus really agreed?"

Eoin nodded. "Aye, *mò gradh*. He said my place is with ye, in tha future."

She sat up higher but couldn't break their physical contact. His bare skin was so warm against her, even through layers, the plaid and his leine. She sighed.

"Somethin' wrong?" He continued to stroke her shoulders and back.

"I just don't know, Eoin—"

"'Tis settled, Ash. *Mò gradh*." His words were an

order, but the delivery playful. He punctuated them with soft kisses all over her face. "Trust yer laird."

Ashlyn grinned; couldn't help it. "Okay."

She loved him. He loved her.

Eoin trusted *her* enough to jump centuries permanently, so she'd have to trust him, too.

He was going to come home with her?

To live?

Her whole body leapt.

Love was easy if it was with Eoin.

chapter nineteen

The bell sounded and roused him. It took Eoin time to orient.

Ah, right.

He was in the twenty-first century, with the most beautiful woman of all time, wrapped around him, gloriously naked. In a place called Dallas, Texas, which was most certainly different than Scotland.

Not just the change of century would take getting used to, but it didn't matter.

As long as he was with Ashlyn.

The repetition of the sound pushed him into action, but he didn't want to disturb his love. *Blinking* across the ocean had tired them both out, but it was better than having to brave what Ashlyn had called an *airplane.*

She'd explained it would take hours upon hours, even though that was the preferred method of travel to her home state of Texas, in what she called, the USA.

Eoin hadn't worn himself out with magic like he'd felt when he'd collapsed on her bed, since he'd been a wee lad. He'd even been too tired to take Ashlyn, although they'd 'Christened her bed'—as she'd called it—in the middle of that first night. Nessie would faint if she heard the misuse of that term. He chuckled and dropped a kiss on Ashlyn's honey locks.

She groaned in her sleep, but he slipped out from under the arm she had across his chest without waking her.

As promised, he'd returned her to when he'd taken her in Inverness — moments after, of course, so they didn't run into themselves. Ashlyn had roused her best friend, and together they'd explained everything to Kate. Convincing her had taken a few hours, and Eoin couldn't swear that the redheaded beauty believed them even now.

They'd remained in modern-day Scotland for the rest of the trip the lasses were on. By the end of the second day, his Ashlyn's friend had told him they had her blessing to be together. Also, that she liked him.

Since it'd meant so much to his love, he'd thanked the fulsome lass. He'd thought Kate a beauty when he'd seen her again, but standing next to his little *seanchaí*, made the redhead's looks pale. No woman was his Ashlyn.

Eoin had even gotten to tour Dunvegan with them. Talk about surreal, seeing his home in a time so different from his own, but he was immensely proud the MacLeod stronghold still stood. It looked vastly different, of course, but it was still his home.

The fake Faery Flag, along with his ancestor Rory Mor MacLeod's horn, and the Dunvegan Cup were all on display, and the Flag looked very much like the real thing—thanks to the witch, Korinna. He'd left the genuine one with his grandfather, and he could only pray it stayed in the eighteenth century.

Despite being a married woman, his little pest hadn't taken to the idea of him leaving, likely permanently. Fiona had cried in his arms, then in Ashlyn's.

The poor lad she'd wed looked lost, as if he didn't know what to do with the sobbing lass, but Kenneth had tried his best to comfort her, too. At least Eoin was confident he'd left his sister in good hands. The lad loved her.

Eoin had promised to visit if it was at all possible, but after *blinking* across the ocean after time traveling, he wasn't keen to do it again, even to see his family. Time would tell. He'd probably get homesick and reevaluate. His Ashlyn wasn't opposed to visiting; more research, she'd joked.

He tugged up what she'd called *basketball shorts* and meandered to her front door. She'd told him she lived in a quiet *neighborhood,* in something that was called a *duplex*. Eoin would learn all the terms sooner or later.

One thing he liked about the twenty-first century was coffee. In Scotland, she'd taught him to make it, and he should do that for her. The machine in her home wasn't so different he couldn't manage it. He would, after he answered the incessant alarm.

A man dressed in brown—complete to his boots

and hat, was on Ashlyn's porch, with a parcel of sorts in his hand. "Hi, can you sign this for me?" he asked, holding up some foreign object the likes of which Eoin had never seen.

Of course, he didn't want to admit that. "Aye. Where?"

The man handed him a round thing that resembled a cigar. "On the dotted line." He pointed with the object before handing it over.

"I've got it," Ashlyn said from behind him.

He turned to see her clad in a light blue robe that stopped mid-thigh. Eoin wanted to growl for her to cover herself, especially when the man at the door perked up and wore a smile.

His love kissed his cheek, and smiled as if she could read his mind, then took the square-like thing from the man, and the stick-like object, jotting her name with it.

Eoin tried not to gasp. It didn't seem like ink. It was more like a *computer screen*. Something else she'd shown him. It wasn't magic, but it appeared like it.

Soon the door was closed, and the gold-colored fat square was in Ashlyn's hands. "It's okay; you'll get the hang of everything. Hey, this is addressed to you."

"'Tis?"

Ashlyn nodded and his heart skipped at the love he read in her dark eyes.

Eoin took the parcel. It was soft, as if padded on the inside. He could indeed see his name written in black, but with what was called, her *address* — the location of her home — under it. No one knew he was here. "What?"

"I dunno, let's open it." She shrugged; her countenance curious.

All manner of small things fell onto the kitchen counter, out of what she called an *envelope*. One was a small rectangle with his image on it.

"What?" he sputtered. Eoin hated to admit he had no idea what he was holding and looked at his love.

Ashlyn gasped. Held a hand over her mouth.

"*Mò gradh?*"

"It's identification. So, you're here legally, and...*present* in the, well, present." She indicated the date thirty years in the past, with the correct day and month of his birth. The year, of course, was three hundred years wrong. "This is called a Green Card, and people who immigrate to the United States need one to be a citizen. They're very hard to get. A real pain in the ass. They don't give them to everyone who wants one." Ashlyn gestured to the whole pile of things he didn't understand. "Even a Texas drivers' license, though I'm not in a hurry to teach you to drive." She flashed a watery smile.

Eoin cupped her cheeks and wiped her tears away, couldn't *not* touch her. "I love ye," he whispered.

"I love you, too. But...how is this possible?"

"I've an idea." He pushed through the items and

found a piece of modern parchment. He'd never get used to its smooth feel or the way people discarded pieces of it as if it wasn't the expensive item, it should be.

Eoin unfolded the letter and read it...twice.

Laird MacLeod,

Glad you found when you're supposed to be. Here's everything you should ever need. Your lady love can explain it to you.
We will meet again someday.
Live your life with love and laughter.

-K

He beamed and handed the letter to Ashlyn.

She gasped as she read it. "But...Eoin..."

"I ken it, *mò gradh*."

"Thank you, Korinna!" Ashlyn threw herself into his arms and peppered kisses all over his face. "I love her! I love her, and I love *you*!"

He chuckled and caught her up, holding her tight and close. Kissed her mouth, darting his tongue inside so he could fully taste her. "We need ta go back ta that big modern bed, lass," Eoin breathed against her lips.

She grinned, then broke into a fit of giggles.

"Somethin' amusin', *mò gradh*?"

"Nothing and everything." Ashlyn shook her

head, her brown eyes dancing. "I didn't have to write a Happily Ever After this time. I finally got one of my own."

the end

about the author

USA Today Bestselling, award winning author of romantic suspense, epic and historical fantasy romance, C.A. loves to dabble in different genres. If it's a good story, she'll write it, no matter where it seems to fit!

She's a hopeless romantic and always will be. Risking it all for Happily Ever After is what she lives by!

C.A. is originally from Ohio, but got to Texas as soon as she could. She's happily married and has a bachelor's degree in Criminal Justice.

She's always writing, and helps small business owners by writing their websites, and she loves it!

WEBSITE: http://www.caszarek.com
EBOOK STORE:
https://www.caszarek.com/ebook-store
PAPERBACK STORE:
https://www.caszarek.com/paperback-store
FACEBOOK:
http://www.facebook.com/caszarek
INSTAGRAM:
https://www.instagram.com/caszarek/
TWITTER: https://twitter.com/caszarek
BOOKBUB:
https://www.bookbub.com/profile/c-a-szarek
GOODREADS:
https://www.goodreads.com/author/show/5815085
.C_A_Szarek
EMAIL: ca@caszarek.com

You can sign up for C.A.'s newsletter on her website, as well as buy all her books!

www.ingramcontent.com/pod-product-compliance
Lightning Source LLC
Chambersburg PA
CBHW050351190726
48284CB00007BB/2236